I0642686

LOVER HUSBAND FATHER

HIS STORY

GRAEME JOHNSTONE

Lover, Husband, Father, Monster
- His Story

Copyright © Graeme Johnstone

G. & E. Johnstone

ISBN: 978-0-9925059-9-8

All rights reserved. No part of this publication may be reproduced in any manner whatsoever, or stored in a retrieval system or transmitted in any form or by any means, electronic, mechanical, photocopying, recording or otherwise, without the prior written permission of the authors, except in the case of brief quotations embodied in critical articles or reviews. Please do not participate in or encourage the piracy of copyrighted materials in violation of authors' rights. Purchase only authorized editions.

The publisher and author assume no responsibility or liability whatsoever on the behalf of any purchaser or reader of this material. Any perceived slight of specific people or organizations is unintentional. While all attempts have been made to verify information provided in this publication, neither the author nor the publisher assumes any responsibility for errors, omissions or contrary interpretation of the subject matter herein.

Thank you for your support. This novel is the second in the trilogy, following *Lover, Husband, Father, Monster – Her Story*, by Elsie Johnstone. If you enjoyed these books, you might wish to read the gripping conclusion: *Lover, Husband, Father, Monster – The Aftermath*, by Elsie and Graeme Johnstone. All three books are available as paperbacks or eBooks from amazon.com, smashwords.com or through online and traditional book retailers.

For more information on these books and other publications go to: www.loverhusbandandfathermonster.com

For children everywhere who suffer because of the choices their parents make.

1

The truth be known, the first time Jennifer and I ever actually touched, I recoiled from her. Considering how things panned out, that action now reeks of the most overwhelming irony. If I had left it at that, followed my usual instincts and moved quietly into the background, our hearts and our souls would never have become so intrinsically intertwined as they did. Rather than a tiny, incidental brush of our hands leading to romance, marriage and children, we would have gone our separate ways, continuing our grinding parallel ride down the gloomy fast track to loneliness. Our lives would have been less productive, less colourful, less meaningful, certainly less complicated and undoubtedly far less tragic. I would never have found myself standing on that motorway flyover with my sleepy little daughter in my arms, the roar of traffic thundering in my ears and a catastrophic surge of blind anger and white-hot fury coursing through my veins.

However, let's be clear. On that first meeting, I did not pull back from Jennifer out of revulsion or fear. Not at all. It was purely out of politeness.

We both had turned and reached for the last sandwich on a plate in the middle of a long serving table. As the occasion was a cup of tea after a very sombre funeral, our reactions were both straight out of the book of good manners, trying to do the right thing. I pulled my hand away and whispered, 'I'm terribly sorry.' She quietly replied, 'No, no, it's all yours, take it.'

That's not the smartest thing to say to someone who had grown up as an only child. I knew my place in the food chain. At the front of the shortest of all possible queues! But I was also brought up to be polite and courteous. And when I looked down and focused on those pretty features surrounded by a beautiful aura of auburn hair, I was intrigued. Instead, I picked up the plate, gave a little bow, and presented it to her as if she was the lady of the manor. 'I am your humble servant, M'am,' I said. I don't usually do quirky things like that. I'm an insurance salesman.

As I peeked up from my subservient position, I could see that although she was reaching for the food, she was peering at me with the most delightful look on her face. Sure, we were at a funeral and the atmosphere was thick with melancholy, but the sparkle in her green eyes re-energized my spirits.

We might have just buried one of my mother's cousin's boys – only 14, he had been knocked over by a motorcyclist wired on coke trying to out-run the Garda in Limerick – but I was beguiled by the cheery laughter in her voice.

We had just been overwhelmed by the tear-stained singing of the young boy's classmates, doing that U2 song about trying to find something they were looking for, but here before me was the most engaging smile, emphasised by brilliant cherry-coloured lipstick. I just had to keep the conversation going. But what to say?

'Poppy,' I blurted. She looked confused. 'Your lipstick. Poppy King, isn't it? She's Australian and the colours are like the country, big and bold.'

She looked down and began pulling her coat tightly across her body. It was red like her lipstick and even I knew that it was very fashionable. I figured she was cold and so I began looking around somewhat helplessly for the controls to the room heating. Then it dawned on me that it was not the cold she was worrying about, rather my mention of the lipstick. It had made her re-consider her outfit. She hastily explained that she had been on her way to work when she had heard about the funeral. 'I guess I should be wearing something more appropriate,' she added, trying to cover the short skirt underneath.

'You're not out of place at all,' I said hesitantly. 'You look … beautiful …'

And that's how it all began. After I had unaccountably uttered those words – in all of my thirty-eight years I had never been so forward with anyone – I felt that if the poor dead boy's grave had opened up before me right there and then, I would have jumped in. But that was the characteristic I was to constantly discover and re-discover about Jennifer. She never got fazed by things like that. She would just tilt her head and smile again, and if the previous smile had been fetching, the next one would be breathtaking. The white, even teeth dazzling through the bright lipstick. She simply leant forward, took my silver-grey mourning tie in both hands, gently pushed the knot up to the top button of my white shirt, patted it down and said, 'You look pretty swish yourself.'

'Blimey,' I replied.

She giggled loudly. 'I haven't heard blimey for years,' she said. 'That's English, isn't it? Cor blimey and all that?'

I explained how I had inherited the expression from my father. How he had been born in Ireland, but went over to England with his migrating family in the 1920s when he was a boy and eventually served in the British Army, picking up a lot of their sayings.

I knew from what Dad had told me and from my history lessons at school that at one stage there were more Irishmen serving in the British Army than Englishmen. But seeing as we were standing in a room in Dublin, the capital of the Republic of Ireland, a country that had not entirely enjoyed its eight hundred years of British rule, this could have elicited any response. Not the least of which might well have been a lecture replete with deep-seated hatred of the English. 'My Mam is also Irish,' I added hastily.

Instead, this pretty young woman standing before me laughed and said that I was quite a combination. 'Irish scattiness sharpened by all-conquering English discipline,' she said. 'So, at the end of the day, which one has come to the fore?'

'I let other people judge that,' I said. 'I just keep my head down, try my hardest and hope for the best outcome. What about you?'

Her eyes looked to the heavens. 'Wow, have we got time?' She laughed. 'The classic Catholic upbringing to start with. With a name like Jennifer Mary O'Brien, what would you expect? But now I'm Buddhist.'

It was my turn to be put off balance. I didn't know much about Buddhism other than what I had seen in the media. Monks praying in orange robes, long-running but unsuccessful resistance to China controlling Tibet, the Dalai Lama turning up to conferences on humility in a

Mercedes. But I had obviously steered things towards her favourite topic. She made the declaration with such a happy lilt in her voice that a group of mourners near us stopped their conversation and turned to see who on earth could be finding something funny about a funeral. I asked her about how she got involved in Buddhism and the answer, quite frankly, was a bit rambling. Something about how she had studied at Cambridge University, which I found most impressive, even a bit daunting, and how she had met a few people there who had something to do with people in Thailand, a very committed Buddhist country, and how she started to appreciate the philosophy and then travel around a bit and meet other people and now she was practicing it. So I asked her how Buddhists worshipped God, and she replied cheerily, 'Oh, we don't necessarily believe in God.'

'You don't believe in God?' I replied loudly. The whole room came to a halt and an elderly man in a blue-serge double-breasted suit with long swept-back silver hair broke away from his group and marched deliberately towards us. He stepped up to me so closely that I could see the tiny pink whiskey veins hatching out of his red bulbous nose. He hissed at us to be quiet. 'The religious beliefs, fanciful or otherwise, of you and your lady friend here are of no interest to anyone, especially at a terrible time like this,' he said.

He nodded at me as if to emphasise his point, turned and looked at Jennifer angrily, then wheeled around abruptly and walked away. I could hear the next giggle welling in her throat, so I lightly took her by the arm and hurried her away from the table towards a quiet corner. I looked down and, to my horror, realised that I was touching her – bustling her along, in fact. To my great joy, she was not resisting. Indeed, here she was, quite happy to come with me, her high heels click-clacking on the polished boards. A surge like an electrical charge went through my body. This had not happened to me for years.

We found a spot by a sickly-looking rubber-plant near a window overlooking the grey, wet, Dublin street below. She looked up at me, giggled once more, then continued unperturbed, saying that she had grown up Catholic and therefore could understand my response.

'But as a Buddhist, God is not an issue for me,' she said.

'I wouldn't want my mother to hear that,' I replied, looking anxiously back towards the room. 'She thinks God plays a significant role in the Church of Ireland. Quite a substantial one, in fact ...'

'Hmm, Church of Ireland!' she said, jumping on the reference to my Protestant upbringing. 'Well, I suppose we're both something of the rebel then.'

She smiled and leaned in close to me. The musky aroma of her perfume – Lulu, I reckoned, based on my experiences with doctor's surgery magazine scratch-and-scent advertisements – was absolutely intoxicating. 'Me, perhaps, a little more than you,' she cheekily added. 'But I'm sure down the track that that won't matter.'

I smiled weakly and put my hand on the window sill to steady myself.

'Blimey,' I whispered, staring straight into her green eyes. 'Blimey.'

2

I t has taken me a very, very long time to appreciate an intriguing fact of life: not everyone is fascinated by the world of insurance.

Why, some people even think it is a bit dreary. That astounds me. I think insurance is a beautiful thing. That's because it is a matter of selling an intangible, a notion, a possibility. And not a lot of people can do that. It requires a level of patience and a touch of guile that not everyone has in them. Over the years, I have observed many of my associates struggling with that challenge. They would join our brokerage with a great track record for selling tangible, touchable products like cars or houses or lawn-mowers but were unable to reproduce that same level of sales success. That's because insurance is based on the possibility of something terrible happening. And I was very good at outlining what the 'something' might be to potential clients.

'Sir,' I would say, 'if something goes wrong, we step in and clean up the mess, pay your bills, get you back on your feet and return things to where they were before. You may even be better off.'

'Sir,' I would add, 'the decision is up to you. I know you're an intelligent, honest, reliable man, who does a good job looking after himself and his family. You never do anything to put yourself at risk. But, what if? You know, what if ..?'

'Sir,' I would continue, ramping things up, 'I don't need to tell you, it's a fast-moving world out there. Anything can happen. Things get out of control. You could get hurt. People are so unpredictable these days, on the drug and all that. Not that I'm saying something like that will happen to you, but you never know. Better to be on the safe side and sleep well at night. That is the question you have to ask yourself: can you sleep well at night?'

Then I would ask him three questions.

'Can you sleep well, knowing that your car is not locked up in a garage, but sitting out in the street, providing some angry young punk, whose mother never breast-fed him and whose father was always at the betting shop, with the perfect opportunity to steal it or smash its windows or torch it for the hell of it?'

'Can you lie back, knowing that you might get laid off one day and the mortgage will still have to be paid? Things are getting very, very tough you know, and those banks, they hold the money, they play with the money, they do what they like with the money, but they never give the ordinary man any of the money.'

'And can you nod off, knowing that although you're healthy now, you will get older and your physical wellbeing will, naturally enough, begin to deteriorate? We all know the statistics; that the husband usually dies before the wife. Wouldn't it be good to know that she'll be financially secure after you've gone? I'm not trying to be morbid here, but you know what I mean, having that warm feeling deep down that you've done the right thing by her.'

That was the game and that's how it went and that's why I liked it. Talking to people about the unthinkable, the unlikeable, the unpredictable – nevertheless, things that we all knew could actually happen – and helping them create a reserve force that they could call on if need be. It was all in the insurer's handbook.

Another reason I liked insurance was that I had endured two other serious 'careers' before I fell in love with the game, both of which were desk-bound, and both soul-destroying. One was spent in the civil service shuffling papers and the other was wasted trying to make sense of patient registrations at a hospital. The first seemed to have no point in it at all while the second involved people constantly whingeing. I hate whingers. So from the moment I joined a small insurance agency and very quickly began successfully selling policies door-to-door, I knew it was for me. Within twelve months I was their top salesman; by the end of three years, I was deputy manager; two years after that I was sitting on the board. Recognising the advantages of running my own business, I persuaded Derek Smythe, another successful operator in the building, to go halves in buying the place out. The owner, Frank Cunningham, the last of the insurer gentlemen, had lost his enthusiasm after his wife had died of a terrible cancer and was only too glad to hand it over to young blood at a modest price.

Above all, I liked selling insurance because people trusted me. They saw me as straight, honest, reliable. The type of person that wouldn't scare the horses or start the dogs barking or do anything crazy and act out of character. I was always polite, I took a great interest in their personal lives and I knew when to drop a line into the conversation with a little dash of humour. I also presented very well. I always wore quality charcoal or blue pin-stripe suits, freshly-pressed white shirts and sombre but expensive ties. I had my hair, which had prematurely turned from a mousey brown to a distinguished grey, trimmed regularly. I wore the latest spectacle frames and made sure that my shoes were polished to a mirror finish every morning. My father's military approach, that you should give off an impressive, commanding image at all times, was well ingrained in me. 'You have to look sharp as a tack,' he would say, circling me as if inspecting a parade, 'whether you're in uniform or wearing mufti.'

I became acknowledged for my presentation and professionalism and got to deal with a lot of people from a broad spectrum of life. Employees, employers, businessmen, businesswomen, housewives, young men and women climbing the executive ladder, even the occasional celebrity. The yuppies were the toughest to crack. They made a lot of money rapidly and spent it just as quickly, mainly on preening, enhancing and amusing themselves with not much thought for the future. They were convinced they were indestructible. Deep down, I will admit, I didn't like their attitude. It took a lot of time and effort, surreptitiously of course, to convince them that their future, so cocky and self-assured as it was then, would need protecting.

Sometimes I also came across artistic, hedonistic characters that made money in large episodic chunks but couldn't control it. They wrote or painted or made music or just 'were'. Things happened to them, good things, and they would laugh and celebrate and people would throw themselves at them. Then bad things would happen to them, and the hangers-on would disappear and I would be left to console these so-called superstars in their helplessness and sort out a plan to get them back on track until the next pile of cash inexplicably surfaced through some flukey project coming off or magically appeared out of the wallet of a star-struck celebrity-seeking benefactor. They were an insurer's and financial planner's nightmare.

Selling insurance therefore required patience, diligence, the ability to remain calm while a potential client pondered the plan so carefully presented. I never got angry or frustrated. Certainly not with customers, anyway. That was my hallmark. People would always comment on my calm, relaxed approach. I guess I was good at burying the frustration deep within me. I bottled it all up but always remained tranquil on the surface, even with something as tricky as marine insurance, when cargo was damaged or stolen or, as happened once, the actual ship disappeared off the face of the earth.

My usually unflappable father would get excited about my job when something like that happened. 'When you say the ship disappeared, do you mean sunk? Or pirates? Or aliens? Or what?' he would ask, twitching his moustache. As an old army man, this was the only aspect of my otherwise apparently humdrum career that fascinated him. There could be an enemy involved and he loved a good enemy. That was because from the broader perspective my job, my approach, my very existence had been a complete disappointment to him. Sure, I had inherited his apparent coolness under pressure – 'a vital part of any good soldier's make-up,' he would tell me – but none of his swagger, will-to-win or bloodlust. I was like Mum. Patient, reserved, staying under the radar. Holding things in, bottling them up. That's how she had handled life while Da's career dragged them from posting to posting, from army camp to army camp, from the same dreary sergeant's quarters to yet another scantily furnished home. I remember a stretch when we occupied half a dozen different places in nine years.

The fact that I was their only child simply added to Dad's aggravation. He had fired the one shot he had in his locker and as far as he was concerned, it had fizzed. I had not become an officer. Hadn't even tried to get into the army. He had seen that as the way for me to make up for his own work-a-day role. After my schooling, he was convinced that I would go to university, get a degree and become a leader of men, directing their every action with cool military precision from the safety of the bunker behind the lines and then heading off to the officers' mess for a brandy with the chaps.

Shifting from school to school did not help my self-esteem much, so on one occasion they tried to break the circuit by enrolling me in a boarding college. In many ways, I liked the place. There was a discipline and a surety about it. You knew what was going to happen and when. There were rituals to be followed and games to be played. The teaching was excellent, albeit brutal at times, and I excelled particularly in the maths and commerce subjects. But apart from developing a friendship with a genial lad named Olaf Hendrikson from Sweden, whose father had been transferred to England on business, it was a very isolating experience for the son of a sergeant amongst the offspring of the officers and the well-to-do. I very quickly ran into the thick brick wall known as the English class system and rapidly learned that name, pedigree and dynasty bore fruit, not necessarily brains, talent and dedication. In the showers, on the playing fields, at the back of the class, I was bullied by over-bearing chinless wonders with hyphenated names. They lampooned me for having a father who was a mere workaday soldier and not an officer and gentleman. They teased me for my so-called lack of class and my mongrel heritage of being born in England but of Irish parents. So, they pushed my head down the toilet bowl and flushed it. They coated my genitals with boot polish. They cut a single sleeve off three of my shirts.

And, of course, they loved my surname of Hoare. In my opinion, Hoare is not such a bad name. It comes from the Old English 'hoar', meaning white or frosty or grey, and amongst the Hoare lineage is a former British Foreign Secretary and an internationally successful computer whiz.

But my tormentors went for the obvious. They couldn't believe their luck that some poor sod had come onto their radar with a surname that matched perfectly with 'whore'. I was therefore the ideal target for adolescent taunts about prostitution. 'Hoare, you fucker, you do it for money,' they would say. Or, 'How many did you sleep with last night, Hoare?' And a chant that they just loved to get going: 'Hoare, the whore, he's got no class. Hoare, the whore, he takes it up the arse.' Looking around the cold, grey-stone dormitories of the English boarding college, ruled by predatory masters, I thought that that was hardly an original attack. Mercifully, I was at least saved from that indignity because – as it dawned on me years later – I innocently undermined any attempts by teachers to inculcate dangerous friendships through my characteristic aloofness. In my own quiet way, I simply hung on, survived and bottled it all up.

The key was to never respond to the gang's bullying taunts. I absorbed their punishment, stored it away and let it simmer.

Then, just when I was starting to make some headway – my stocky build earning me a place in the rugby squad and a modest talent for music securing me the role of piano accompanist for the choir – it happened. One of the thugs pushed me too far. But he made the grave mistake, perhaps being too cocky, of being by himself this time and not backed up by the rest of the group. 'So, if your father is a Hoare, is your mother a whore, too?' he sneered. This mention of my mother in that context was too much. I snapped. The simmering anger, subdued for nearly two years, burst to the surface in an uncontrollable rage. I flew at him and, even though he was several centimetres taller and a few kilos heavier than me, I caught him flush on the jaw with a wild, round-house, bar-room brawl swing.

As he dazedly toppled to the ground, shocked and momentarily disoriented, I jumped on him, pinning him down with my knees on his shoulders, and started flailing into him with lefts and rights. I could feel the stinging pain in my knuckles and hear the sound of ripping flesh as I smashed my fists into the side of his head, onto the bridge of his nose, down the side of his jaw, and around his eyes. Months and months of bottled up anger was let free in one breathtaking, vicious assault. It was like another person had taken over.

For once in my life, I felt enormous power and control as I belted into him, his pleas for me to stop drowned out by the shouts of a group of kids who had gathered around, many of whom were thrilled to see this thug finally cop the punishment he deserved.

Their noise eventually attracted the attention of one of the masters and I was pulled off, giving him one final salute, a kick in the balls, as they dragged me away. My tormentor was battered and bruised, shaken and humiliated, his face and shirt covered in blood, his left eye closing, as they hurried him off to the infirmary. It was my one great triumph in the school yard but it was also my downfall. In the inquisition that followed, class distinction and aristocratic pressure won out. I was expelled, while my tormentor and his cronies survived and went in search of another innocent target. I heard later that they found him in the son of an aspirational lorry-driver named Whitcombe. It turned out I was considerably luckier than him. After two terms of relentless torment, he went into the groundsman's shed at the bottom of the playing fields, swallowed half a bottle of weed-killer and found blessed relief through a most horrible death.

My mother insisted that we never speak about this extraordinary blow-up again, although my father was secretly pleased that I had shown such gumption. I was left to ponder whether such an outburst of violence would ever happen again and, if so, what sort of circumstances would be needed to trigger it. The incident was quietly written out of the family history and I was soon back to the same old education treadmill, tramping from school to school and finally getting my A levels. It was years before I got any tertiary qualifications, having to go through night school when we moved back to Ireland. My entry-level diplomas in finance and business came from slogging away at work during the day and sitting through endless classes in the evenings.

In some ways, it was a pity the boarding school opportunity collapsed, because my parents had tried so hard to ensure that I would not be a poorly-educated, poorly-paid hireling like Dad was, exposed in the field, shouting at indolent foot-sloggers and keeping them in line. He had done that in North Africa, Greece and

Burma during the war, before finishing up in India, where he and Mum had hung on after independence for as long as they could before my impending arrival forced them to return.

I don't think that it ever helped his demeanour that they had finally settled in Ireland, Mum's place of birth, rather than England, where he was brought up and for whom he had so faithfully served, even though he, too, was Irish born. When he finally retired on his diminutive army pension, he would stride around the tiny flat on the outskirts of Dublin, peering out the window, waiting for the enemy to appear. No one came. No enemies. No friends, either. Pulling on the uniform of the nation that had once occupied the country was a reasonable means to an end for some Irish but unforgivable as far as many others were concerned. He cut a lonely figure huddled over his whiskey in the pub at the end of the street.

Sometimes, in moments of melancholic reflection, he spoke about his experiences in the war. The circumstances had to be right; a wandering mind, a few too many drinks and a sound or smell.

It was the tale of the German soldier that he had bayoneted in a little village they were fighting over in the battle of Crete that would bring the tears to his eyes. 'Only a boy,' he would say. 'I surprised him from behind and he turned, yanking his revolver out of his holster, aiming straight at me and pulling the trigger. But it jammed. The gods of war move in strange ways. He threw the pistol at me and turned to run, tripping on the rough stone. As he lay sprawled on the ground, I plunged the bayonet into him. Once, twice, three times. Had to save my ammunition.'

Then he would stop and vacantly stare into the distance and the tears would roll down his face. 'I was doing my job but he was only a boy,' he would mutter, shaking his head. 'He was only a boy. And so was I …'

Mum and I always knew it was senseless to try and comfort him. She would busy herself around him, silently plumping the cushions on the sofa and dusting the mantelpiece while I would look around the room quietly, waiting for him to bring himself back into the present.

There was not a lot about that in the insurer's handbook.

LOVER, HUSBAND, FATHER, MONSTER

3

As an only child, I grew up a lonely child. Until I met Jennifer, making female friends had proved to be an extremely difficult process for me.

I would make tentative, awkward steps to draw a girl into friendship but I never had the confidence or the wherewithal to, for want of a better phrase, go in for the kill. It used to frustrate me to see flashy fellows at work with half a brain chatting up girls and getting them to smile, then giggle, then agree to go out with them, all in a matter of minutes. How did they do that? When I tried the same approach, I would run up against a brick wall.

At work or with a group down the pub at the end of the week, my conversation aimed at asking someone out was always a set piece that I had pre-prepared in my ordered mind, carefully rehearsed with a clear target at the end. But if the girl deviated from the script, I would lose the plot quickly and withdraw in disarray, a tongue-tied, nervous wreck. There was no more frightening experience for a young man than facing up to a group of girls standing in a tight little tribe, no greater challenge than trying to ask one of them out, and no more embarrassing sensation when it all goes pear-shaped and he turns and walks away, the sound of only slightly smothered, hand-over-the-mouth snorting ringing in his burning ears.

Such was my fragile, nervous state, my first ever serious girlfriend, a young woman named Patricia, used to psychoanalyse me. She would plumb the depths of Freud when we got into discussion about the importance of 'self' as our spluttering romance blossomed in chaotic fashion. 'There's an entire seminar on the development of single-cell existence in you,' she would exclaim.

I had been attracted to Patricia because she looked like my mother. Short, brunette with deep brown eyes and an enigmatic smile. But I soon learned I was going out with my father. Under the benign camouflage lurked not just a sergeant, rather a camp commandant. She was incredibly decisive, insistent and powerful. Few people could get a lazy restaurant waiter hopping like Patricia could, or castigate a Garda and get the speeding ticket torn up, or belittle someone who had carelessly thrown an empty beer bottle onto the footpath. And in her role as a publicist or marketer or event manager – whatever it was, I could never quite get a grip on it – I think she took me on as a challenge. It was the *Pygmalion* scenario, albeit in reverse; her Henry Higgins to my Eliza Doolittle. And it was perhaps not so much my accent that she wanted to change, rather that I would actually speak up in the first place.

In those early days, the only people I spoke to with any confidence were my mother, my male work-mates and myself – the latter when no one else was looking, I might point out. In social situations, when faced with discussion with other people, I tended to reply with polite but nevertheless monosyllabic responses of the 'yes' and 'absolutely' variety. 'He's a nice young man,' they would whisper to each other, not quite out of earshot, 'but he's very quiet.'

Patricia did have some success in getting me to speak up. The first time she undressed before me, I uttered 'Good heavens', and at the apex of us making love, I exclaimed 'Blimey'. Seeing as I had just made love to a real live person for the first time, seven weeks and five days after my twenty-third birthday, I felt that something strong was needed. So, 'Blimey' it was.

Patricia was not so impressed. I never saw her again.

Thus wounded, it took me another two years to establish a relationship. And this time, with Tanya, things moved quite a bit down the track. She was blonde, she was blue-eyed, she was beautiful. As well, Tanya was less predatory than Patricia, something I relished after such a long period of regaining my confidence to approach a girl again. In fact, if anything, the roles were reversed. Whereas I had been the work in progress with Patricia, I found myself taking the lead in Project Tanya. If it was at all humanly possible, Tanya was less sure-footed than me. 'Golly', I thought, 'if my father was a sergeant, then her Dad must have been in the Marines. She's been ground totally into the dirt.'

She was like a deer stuck eternally before the headlights, the product of a broken marriage, a sporadic education and some deeply hidden secret that I never really unearthed. We sort of meandered into romance - we went to movies, ate at cheap Turkish restaurants and visited tiny art galleries off O'Connell Street exhibiting works by moody artists obsessed with death - and then we sort of meandered out of it again.

I started to notice the extraordinary number of bottles of pills in her handbag. They rattled like the Queen Mother's jewellery. She became vaguer and vaguer and her pretty looks began to harden. One day a phone conversation about meeting up to see a film – she wanted to see *Kramer vs. Kramer,* the big weepy of that year, while I was pushing for *The China Syndrome,* which had more of a political edge – slowly trailed off. My closing farewell, 'I'll talk to you later', was never fulfilled. I was mortified the next time I saw her. Or at least, the photo of her in the newspapers. Her face was puffed, there were dark circles around her lifeless eyes and her once shining blonde hair hung like limp, lank string. How she got the energy much less the wherewithal to try and rob a Post Office I will never know. The judge was similarly bemused, particularly as her weapon of befuddled choice was a blunt table knife. He mercifully ordered a suspended sentence, detoxification and clinical care rather than a stint in gaol.

Dad just ticked this experience off as yet another failure on my part while Mum wrung her hands, praying and hoping that the right girl would turn up one day. After the searing experiences of Patricia and Tanya, it was a long, long time before I ventured into the world of romance again, and I vowed that if I did, I would play things very cautiously.

4

With a woman like Jennifer, things were totally different. Maybe it was because we were both mature adults. Perhaps it was because we met in such a strange and unlikely setting. Either way, our relationship got off to a good start. At the funeral, my interaction with her was spontaneous. There had been no time for preparation. Instead of scripted words, I had to think on my feet and for once the natural me just shone through. At least I think it did, and I hope that that was what attracted her.

Afterwards we slipped away to a dark little bar just down the street. I had a South African chardonnay while she pointed out that alcohol was not really her scene and ordered a lime, soda and ice which came in a tall, thin glass. 'Wow,' I thought, 'she is naturally vivacious, doesn't need any artificial stimulant.' We told each other about ourselves and laughed and philosophised and I had a second glass of wine.

I will never forget that hour or so at the bar. It was one of the most thrilling times of my life, a most absorbing memory being that when she put her glass down, she left a huge cherry-red lipstick mark in the perfect shape of her lips on its rim. As we left, the careful insurance man in me was briefly abandoned. I was so taken by the glass, I stole it. While she was organising her coat and - I fervently hoped - no one else was watching, I slipped it into my overcoat pocket. When I got home that night, I sat the glass on the coffee table, flopped into a chair and just sat there, smiling and happily staring at the outline of her lips.

I couldn't believe my luck. So much so, that a couple of days later, without feeling the usual sense of forboding and dread, I phoned her and asked her if she would like to meet up for a drink, and she said yes. After a coffee in a city café, we went for a stroll through the beautiful grounds of Trinity College and as we walked past the library where people were still queuing up to see the Book of Kells, I was almost floating on air.

Things moved rapidly, and one night after a marvellous dinner – not at a cheap restaurant as with my previous romances, but at Thornton's, the upmarket fish place, then in Portobello Road – she peered up at me as we said goodnight and gave me a look that melted my soul. It was a look that I had never seen in a woman before, other than in the movies. Her eyes were soft and glistening, yet focused right on me. She dropped her head slightly in a delicate movement, her chin dipping down toward her breast. Then she peeked up at me, appealing, beguiling. After a few seconds, she stood up on her tippy-toes and gently kissed me, stepped back and looked at me again. Not a word was spoken. There did not need to be. Typically, I had remained a little reserved up until then. I wanted to be sure of one point; was this for real? But that moment, that look, that kiss convinced me that it was. About a month later, after a meal, a night at the theatre and a double whiskey for me, we ended up in bed. 'Blimey,' I said, as we came to a crashing climax. 'Blimey.'

I was in love. Absolute, genuine, for-certain love. I had found someone who actually seemed to appreciate me for being me. And I wanted her body, mind and soul for me and no one else.

The beauty of it was that there was no giggling behind hands this time, or nasty commands and vitriolic comments, or airy-fairy notions going nowhere. She was beautiful, she was quirky, she was delightful and she was mine. 'Hoare,' I said to myself in the mirror one morning, 'you lucky, lucky man, you! At the tender age of thirty-eight, you have pulled off a miracle! She is absolutely gorgeous. What have you done to deserve this?'

I wanted to go and shout out loudly in the street that I was indeed a fortunate man. I wanted to trawl through the old boys' contact list from my boarding college days and phone up the thugs that had made my life so miserable and say to them, 'So, who's laughing now, you bastards?' I wanted to take her around and show her off to the money makers in the upmarket restaurants of Dublin 4; to the students and grafters in the noisy back streets of Temple Bar; to the busy shoppers in bustling Grafton Street. Instead, I took her to a judo match in Cork.

It was just that I was getting involved in the martial arts at the time. To my few friends and associates, taking up judo seemed an odd choice for a quite, unassuming insurance salesman in his late thirties spooked by the war experiences of his father. But it was the discipline and philosophy of it that appealed to the insurance man in me. Like insurance, you go through a lot of training and preparation in judo; like insurance, you are fully prepared to step in and take action when something goes wrong;

and like insurance, you hope that it won't. Besides, I figured it would help keep me fit. So when I saw the advertisement in the local paper, I made the phone call to the little club in the Liffey Valley and booked my first lesson.

A small bonus was that even Dad liked me for taking it on, in his typically oblique sort of way. While he viewed it as a ridiculous Japanese concept – 'Silly little Asian buggers running around in their pyjamas going chop-socky' – he concluded that at least it had a bit of aggression in it, which appealed to his military upbringing. 'Now you can stand up to anyone who's having a go at you,' he said enthusiastically, 'rather than letting them walk all over you.'

Jennifer became similarly intrigued with the concept of me going into combat. 'Do you get a thrill when you belt your opponent?' she asked cheekily. I tried to explain that it was not really about 'belting' people. It was more a philosophy, a cultural thing, a way of going about your life. 'You're a Buddhist, you should understand,' I said.

'Buddhism does not include any form of violence or physical attack,' she replied, with a firm level of conviction. 'Even the monks in Tibet pursue non-violent protest against the Chinese takeover of their country.'

I explained how judo was more about defence, about disabling the other person. Grappling with them, deflecting their attack and bringing the exchange to a rapid end. 'You don't sink a steel-capped boot in him like some Limerick thug,' I said. 'Judo means "the gentle way".'

She giggled, squeezed the biceps in my left arm with one hand while putting the other to my forehead. 'I get it. The thinking man's fighter,' she said. 'Isaac Newton meets John Rambo.' That was the disarming thing about

Jennifer. The chirpy laugh and the rapid summary of the situation that left you disarmed.

After a just a few lessons, my coach, an ancient stalwart of the game named Len, reputed to have represented Ireland at the Tokyo Olympics, concluded that I was ready for competition and entered me in a big Bank Holiday weekend event in Cork. I said to Jennifer it would be wonderful if she could come along. She frowned as she watched me pack my judogi, the traditional white uniform. 'Isn't it a bit early to be testing yourself against others?' she asked. 'You've only been doing it a few months.'

I said that I figured that I had to start somewhere and was heartened by the fact that I, along with my classmates, had been graded for the competition and therefore would be up against someone of similar skill.

'It's not the level of skill I'm worried about,' she said. 'Have you seen how big they are down there in Cork? Those Munster fellows that play rugby? My brothers have been up against some of them and they're gigantic!'

Two days later I found out what she meant. When I walked to the centre of the mat to bow to my first opponent, I nearly wet my judogi. Opposite me was a Belgian Blue bull cleverly disguised as man. His barrel chest split his uniform to the navel, the yellow sash – signifying that, like me, he was at one of the lower grades – barely lashing it to his waist. Hairy muscled forearms the size of legs of lamb peeked out from the loose sleeves, at the end of which wore gnarled, work-scarred hands with fingers that resembled jumbo bratwurst. When we went back to the edge of the mat to start the bout, he squatted on his massive thighs, grinning through his bushy beard as if he was going to actually enjoy killing me. At a rough estimate, I figured he weighed 120 kilograms, about half my size again. This was not going to be fun.

From the start, the big fellow rushed headlong at me and I called on God to forgive me for all my transgressions. Don't know if that is in the insurer's handbook, but my mother would have liked the concept. He grabbed me, threw me to the ground and got me in a joint lock. I don't think I have ever tapped the mat as quickly to show submission as at that moment.

He got off me, stepped back and smiled. As the referee pulled me up and gently headed me in the general direction of my very patient teacher, I vowed that this would be my last fight. But no. 'Good lad, great learning experience,' said Len, patting me on the back. 'Next bout in forty minutes. See if you can be a little more, ah, aware, next time.'

If it was possible, my second fight was finished in even quicker time and was more embarrassing. In this bout, my opponent was not at all bulky but instead tall, slim and elegant. He was also extremely calm, well balanced and very talented. He stared at me coolly as I mentally went over my game plan. 'Whatever you do,' Len had warned me, 'don't go to his left and let him get you on his hip.' The bout started, I moved toward him, went straight to his left and let him get me on his hip …

Why is it, like a moth to a flame, that the thing we so determinedly promise ourselves we will never do, we then go and do?

He flashed a grin as I hurried obediently into his trap, flicked me over and landed me on the floor in an un-winnable position. The referee declared it all over, after just one deft move, to the sniggers and polite clapping of the audience.

By my third and final match the crowd had almost doubled, enhanced by whispers to go and see 'this eedjit from Dublin who doesn't last more than two feckin' seconds.' In the west, they love sticking it to the city slickers, whether it's judo, football, hurling or drinking pints.

One look at my final opponent and I figured two seconds was an optimistic prediction. If my first challenger had been big, then this man was massive. The stadium shook as he climbed onto the mat and the crowd went wild, baying for blood. Rather than exhibiting typical judo humility, he waved his arms and whipped everyone into a frenzy, like Mohammed Ali before a fight.

As he lumbered straight at me, I did the only thing a wise man would do. I jumped to one side and got out of his way. He kept going in a straight line and shot past me, trying to stop himself at the edge of the mat before crashing into the spectators.

He turned, the look in his eye even angrier, and rushed straight at me, this time catching me front on. I expected him to turn to one side and put me down. But he didn't. And obviously couldn't. He kept coming at me, pushing me out of bounds, causing the judge to pull us apart and start again. I thought, 'This is sumo, not judo! He's only able to come in a straight line.'

Jennifer was on the money when she mentioned Isaac Newton. What did he say? For every action, there is an equal and opposite reaction?

As my enraged opponent charged at me, I stood deliberately and provocatively still. He crashed into me again, not deviating from his line. Perfect, sir, welcome to the world of the mild mannered insurance representative. Grabbing the lapels of his judogi, I let myself fall backwards, stuck my feet forcefully into his stomach, yanked as hard as I could and kicked as high as possible. The force of his motion kept him hurtling over my head. In a beautiful display, he completed an exquisite somersault in the air and landed flat on his back. I could hear the groans as he thudded onto the mat. The crowd went wild, the referee giving me a wink as he helped me get up. 'Not exactly text book,' he whispered as he declared me the winner, 'but effective.'

Len shook his head in disbelief. My opponent's handlers carried him off as he writhed in pain and clutched at his shoulder, which proved to be dislocated. 'God,' I thought, 'wasn't that great? That'll show them not to mess with Stuart.' Jennifer rushed to meet me. 'Clever boy,' she said. 'Newton's Third Law, with a bit of Sylvester Stallone thrown in.'

That night, as we ate our special treat of haddock and chips at Fishy Fishy in the beautiful port of Kinsale, acknowledged by just about every guide book as the best seafood restaurant in all of Ireland, every muscle and joint in my body was racked with pain. So, if my endeavours in the third bout were courageous, then I thought my efforts in getting down on one knee and proposing were simply heroic.

Yes, I asked Jennifer to marry me. It had only been a matter of a few months, but I was in love and the careful insurance man in me told me that it was the right thing, a sure thing, the proper thing. Out of the blue, I just asked her there and then. I wanted her for myself.

By now we had driven up to the old fort overlooking Kinsale's spectacular bay after a few drinks at The Spaniard Hotel where they played the fiddle and sang songs about the infamous 1601 siege of the town which had fully stamped English control on Ireland. The wind coming up from the sea rustled her beautiful auburn hair and she looked down at me kneeling on the cliff-top grass.

'Stuart Hoare, you wild thing, you crazy, crazy man, do you mean it?'

'I wouldn't have it any other way,' I said solemnly.

'Good,' she said. 'So, where's the ring, then?' And she burst into a joyous peal of laughter that only made me more happy and confident in my decision.

In my haste, and this shows the effect she had imparted on the otherwise controlled purveyor of financial services, there was one thing significant missing. The ring. But I did have a few spare loops on my key-ring, one of which I spiralled off and solemnly slid on her finger, making her laugh even more. We resolved the issue the next morning, finding a quaint little silversmith's shop in town. The ring we bought was exquisite; an original design, hand-made by a craftsman, who if I remember correctly, was Welsh. With a large diamond surrounded by four smaller ones in an asymmetrical shape, it not only captured the beautiful feel of Kinsale but it also encapsulated our love.

I might have been wracked with pain from my bouts with Cork's finest and biggest, I might have won only one match out of three, but right at that point, I was the victor. The happiest man on earth.

LOVER, HUSBAND, FATHER, MONSTER

5

T he most enduring memory I have of our wedding is the disbelieving looks on the faces of my family as we assembled for the proceedings. Coming from the deeply conservative Protestant ethic of the Church of Ireland, they were somewhat under-prepared for a Celtic Buddhist ceremony under the full moon of the summer equinox in a Roscommon forest by the banks of the Shannon.

But that is what Jennifer wanted, and I wanted her so much, so who was I to argue?

My mother's usually cosy smile straightened into thin lips as we embarked on the gentle walk from the restored 18th century mansion through the manicured gardens into the woods. Dad – who up until then had been so supportive of what was happening between me and Jennifer because I think in some strange way she reminded him of his mother – muttered dark predictions that any marriage based on 'this Merlin the Magician madness' was doomed.

Fortunately, there were only half a dozen family members on my side to get concerned. Historically, our lineage had not been enthusiastic breeders. When we had been preparing the invitation list, I had suggested that anyone on even the remotest edges of our circle, as long as they could get a decent haircut and present in a suitable outfit, be press-ganged into attendance. That ended up being Mum and Dad, Mum's cousin and her husband, both still very bruised from the death of their son, plus their daughter Mary. Our party was rounded out by my business partner, Derek, and my good friend and trusted insurance valuer and consultant, Buchanan, plus a handful of other friends and assorted acquaintances, including Olaf Hendrikson, one of my very few valued mates from my boarding college days. Olaf, a smart, very loquacious sort of fellow and loved by all, had kept in contact with most of our former classmates. So I felt good having him there, knowing that he would pass the word around the old boys' fraternity, even to those thugs who had given me a hard time, that 'Hoare the Whore' had made something of himself, including marrying this most astonishing, beautiful, vibrant woman.

My group contrasted with Jennifer's colourful, noisy tribe, and I use that word in the nicest possible way, who gathered in their dozens, even though she had said it would be a 'small and exclusive' gathering. Typically, they all turned up whether they had sent back an RSVP or not, and many went with the flow when they spotted the suggestion of 'appropriate dress' on the invitation. Whereas my group were suitably but sombrely dressed in outfits that were clean, neat and could have just as easily been serviceable at a funeral, Jennifer's mob was a fascinating, rolling cartwheel of colour and flair. Even the most mature turned up in robes and saris reflecting the Buddhist ethic or in tunics, tops and leggings in keeping with the Celtic theme. There were layers and layers of thin white cotton billowing in the slight evening breeze, yards of saffron robes, headbands holding together even the most greying of thatches, thick-strapped leather sandals and baggy trousers held up by multi-coloured scarves. They moved amid a constant rattle and chime of bangles, bracelets and necklaces. If the Dalai Lama himself had have pulled up in the Benz to join the throng, no one would have been remotely surprised.

Memories of his Indian times came flooding back for Dad when he spotted the page boy dressed in a green outfit of trousers, waist-coat and turban. Several of Jennifer's little nieces floated around excitedly in green dresses with angel wings attached to their backs. As we headed down the path, the crowd seemed to grow bigger and noisier, our way being made clear by attendants carrying torches that crackled in the balmy summer air. We reached a clearing by the banks of the river and gathered in a circle under the mystical, bright light of the full moon. 'I've been reading that this is where they keep reporting all those UFO sightings,' Mum whispered to Dad.

What happened after that is a bit of a blur. Celtic Buddhism is a strain of the philosophy that was begun by an American guru in the 1970s, the view being the Celtic concepts of mythology and sorcery run more or less parallel with Buddhist contemplation of the meaning of life, both seeking infinite wisdom. As a result of this quirky combination, in that beautiful clearing under the sparkling moonlight, we exchanged vows before a priestly figure named Davina adorned in silver and purple robes. Quite frankly, I would have married Jennifer in the back bar of Dan Foley's pub in Youghal if she had wanted to.

Everything was done in the original language of the Celts. I had rehearsed assiduously in the weeks beforehand to remember my lines and get them right. The energy from the crowd was palpable. When I looked like I was going to stumble on any of the words, their positive life-force lifted me over the line.

So after Davina declared that we, Stuart Richard Hoare and Jennifer Mary O'Brien, were now man and wife, I turned to kiss my new bride and felt a sensation of utter relief combined with pure joy. She had chosen a simple outfit, the lightest of light green, sleeveless, slightly billowing and tied at the waist, and on that night, under the full moon of June 23, 1991, as the summer solstice was about to herald a beautiful new beginning, my Jennifer looked a goddess. Her glorious red hair, rolling down to her shoulders in carefully-prepared ringlets, picked up a silver-tinged aura from both the moonlight and from her jewellery – long, dangling ear-rings which featured the traditional yin and yang Buddhist motif and a broad silver bangle on her left wrist etched with ancient Celtic symbols. Her green eyes sparkled and in keeping with the simple tradition, she wore little make-up and none of her favourite Poppy King lipstick. This, to me, only served to highlight her natural beauty. I was smitten. I wanted her to stay that way forever.

As we all walked back for the reception, sited in a cobbled courtyard amid a circle of flares, even my family began to unwind. Mum concluded that, odd as the ceremony had been and far removed from the concepts of the Church of Ireland, it still had a nice feel about it. She was made to feel even more relieved when she was informed that underneath the purple and silver outfit, Davina was actually a legally registered marriage celebrant and not a daughter of Satan. Everything was legitimate or, as Dad put it, using an old army expression he had picked up in India, 'tickety-boo.'

Whatever it was, Mum figured it was grand because I was now legally married and had a partner for life, something she had yearned for across the years. Seeing as I was now nearly forty, she was a very happy mother. Her smile got broader and broader throughout the night because she was finally fulfilling one of her major wishes. I know my social awkwardness and occasional forays into disastrous romances had pained her greatly and there were times when she thought that marriage for me would never come to pass. She never said it directly to me over the years, but I knew that in her heart that this was really all she wanted. Her references had always been well-meaning but transparently unsubtle, such as, 'There's a new family that has joined the church congregation. They seem very nice, especially their daughter.' Or, 'A good woman does wonders for a man.' And now, that good woman had appeared.

To make things absolutely perfect, Dad also discovered that the celebrations would accommodate all Celtic traditions including the drink. Once a single malt whiskey was thrust in his hand by a waiter dressed as a tribal chieftain, all concern about the bizarre nature of the ceremony was gone. When the Irish fiddle, squeezebox and bodhran were cranked up by the band and we danced by the light of the moon and the flickering flames of the flares for hours on end, Dad sat on a chair at the edge of the circle with a smile that got broader and broader throughout the evening as the music got faster and the staff plied him with more grog. And even if there was only a handful of guests from our side, my trusty valuer Buchanan in his inimitable style made up for our lack of numbers with a vintage performance on the dance-floor. Proving to everyone that not all insurance salesmen are stolid, dreary types, he reeled, rolled, and rocked with his wife, with my new wife, with my mother, with Jennifer's mother, with anyone who wanted to strut their stuff.

At one stage he whispered in the band leader's ear, gathered all the little ones in their pretty dresses and outfits and started a conga line to the music, which eventually collected most of the adults and we weaved our way in and around the tables and trees and flares amid raucous laughter and singing. At the end, Buchanan climbed on a table with a pint, held it aloft and declared a toast. 'To Stuart and Jennifer,' he shouted, 'starting much bloody later than the rest of us, but may they have a wonderful life together.' The responding roar echoed through the forest and across the grasslands.

We had booked out the entire recently-refurbished mansion for the whole wedding party to stay, so no one had to rush off, rather they could sleep in the newly renovated servants' quarters. As we were miles away from anywhere, the music blasted into the early hours and when Jennifer and I finally collapsed on the bed in the bridal suite, formerly the bedroom of the master of the house, we were spent. We flopped on the four-poster, sank into the lush mattress, embraced, kissed … and slept. My last recollection is of rolling over and seeing a painting on the wall opposite. It was of a little girl, aged about five, with reddish hair and beautiful green but quite sad eyes, her face tinged with a state of melancholy, as if she was lost. It was unsigned and had no caption or indicator who she was, so presumably it was a print that the new owners of the house had bought as part of a job lot to decorate the place. Perhaps it was a reaction to such a long day, or the many champagnes, wines and whiskies that I had drunk, but the little girl's sad eyes seared into me, in an almost scary, foreboding manner.

In the morning, I awoke and those eyes were still staring at me, forming a powerful image that was later to come back and haunt me. I turned away and said nothing to Jennifer, as we packed and headed off to Dublin for a night in a hotel, where at last we made genuine love – real, enjoyable, man-and-wife-for-the-first-time 'Blimey' love – and then set off for our honeymoon.

Going to Bermuda was not only my idea, but my little secret, revealed only at the very end. For weeks before, Jennifer had tried to tease the location out of me. She attempted to seduce it from me one night with a bottle of chilled Portuguese rose and my favourite hot curry, but I would not bend, only reluctantly admitting under intense pressure and much tickling that our mystery destination was 'beside the seaside,' was 'terribly English' and started with 'B'.

'The bastard's taking me to Bognor Regis,' I overhead her laughingly say to a friend on the phone one night, which caused me considerable amusement and only added to her curiosity.

The best part was that not only had I secured an excellent flights-and-accommodation package but I had sealed two big insurance deals in the weeks leading up to the wedding and with the handsome royalties was able to upgrade us to a bigger apartment in Nassau, overlooking the beach. The Carribean weather was perfect, the food was brilliant and the water-sports were fantastic.

Jennifer even agreed that my hint that the place was 'terribly English' had some merit, even though the island chain had gained independence from Britain in the 1970s. They still spoke English, called themselves The Commonwealth of Bermuda and played 'God Save The Queen' at official functions.

But, oddly enough, she didn't concede much else. Or contribute that much, either, preferring to stay in the apartment most times while I headed for the beach. She was listless for most of the seven days. No doubt from the pressure and stress of it all, I figured, which was a real pity.

I plunged under the sparkling waves, my pink flesh surfacing wet and salty, and I could not have felt happier. We had been married by the light of the moon and now we were going to enjoy our time in the sun.

6

J ennifer's family was the absolute opposite of mine, not only in number but attitude. While on my side there was me, Mum, Dad, and a handful of occasionally seen relatives, Jennifer not only had her parents but four older brothers and a seemingly endless host of aunts, uncles, cousins, nieces and nephews stretching across several generations. If my family was a planet with a couple of moons, then her lot was the entire Milky Way, an extraordinary collection of heavenly bodies whirling, gyrating and streaking across the sky, stretching to infinity and beyond.

You couldn't fault their graciousness and well-meaning. Whenever we gathered, the women constantly fluttered around me, filling me with endless cream cakes, jam scones and hot cups of tea. They would pump me for information about my family and praise me to the high heavens for being the knight in shining armour who had ridden into Jennifer's life on his valiant steed at such a crucial moment, thus saving her from spending the rest of her life languishing on the shelf, which to them seemed to be a fate worse than death. In between, they talked ceaselessly about babies, children, food, recipes, schools, mothers groups and their well-meaning, boisterous but quite often ineffective husbands.

The raucous babble as they gathered in groups at family functions was matched by the waving, nodding and gesticulating as each endeavoured to get their word in. Somehow, six conversations could be conducted at once between five people and no one would miss a beat. Coming from my discreet little clan, they were an eye-opener to me; beautiful women, mothers, grandmothers and mothers-to-be, with a wonderful humanity and insight into the human existence. I don't think they appreciated just how savvy they were. Or if they did, they did not have time to stop and evaluate it. Caring, generous, concerned, joyous, enthusiastic, they took me in, made me one of the family and fed me up.

With the men, it was a bit different. Jennifer was the only girl in the family and despite their outward friendliness and enthusiasm, her father, Seamus, and four brothers – Patrick, Daniel, Brendan and Kevin – still gave off the air that no one was ever going to be good enough for their much-loved princess. Kevin in particular was the one to be wary of. He was next in age up the line from Jennifer and saw it as his duty to protect his little sister at all times. Just in what way he saw that role, whether it be morally, spiritually or physically, was not clear, least of all to him. But if he felt he detected something or somebody looming on the horizon that would cause her grief, then he would march out, jaw set, eyes narrowed and guns at the ready to see the miscreant off.

The five of them, Jennifer's father included, were all big chaps, gregarious, with florid cheeks and a ready joke, a wink and a laugh. They constantly slapped me on the back, poured pints down my throat whether I wanted them or not and worked diligently at trying to deconstruct my Protestantism and re-create me in the Catholic mould. They endlessly took the mickey out of me because of my strait-laced approach, reactive thinking and cautious contributions at family get-togethers. I suppose I did not help matters with my predilection for writing letters to the more serious newspapers, publicly outlining my opinion on current events, proffering a view that I will readily admit was rather conservative, and which Jennifer regularly described as 'fuddy-duddy.' I was astonished that the boys read anything other than *The Sunday World*, but sure enough, after one of my considered opinions would be published in say, *The Independent* or *The Irish Times*, on the lack of discipline in modern schools or the dissolution of social etiquette or some similar topic, they would be on to it like a shot. 'So, we are all disappearing down the sewer of moral turpitude, are we, Stu?' they would say. Or, 'By God, Stu, you are right, society has reduced itself to the level of the chimpanzee.'

Sometimes, they would call me 'Bertie,' which at first I thought was a friendly jest at my admiration for Bertie Ahern, the Prime Minister who I considered was leading the country out of ingrained poverty into glorious prosperity. Then one day I discovered they meant it as a short form of 'Bertrand,' as in Bertrand Russell, the philosopher. 'No doubt about it, Bertie,' they would say, 'you're the thinking man's thinker.'

I copped all this with an array of silent smiles, false laughter and the occasional riposte, but knew that no matter how hard I tried, I would never be fully part of the O'Brien clan. As I was coming out of the upstairs bathroom of the family home one day I heard Patrick, standing at the foot of the stairs, say to his father, 'He's a nice poor bugger, but he's a bit of feckin' goody two-shoes, isn't he?'

Another time, when I was retrieving a plate of food and a bottle of wine from the back of the car as we arrived for a family lunch, I spotted Seamus out of the corner of my eye standing on the broad patio of their beautiful Blackrock home, giving me the slightly bemused look of a man who was pleased that at last his daughter had settled down, but not entirely convinced that her choice had been the right one. Seamus was originally a Kerry man, a true son of 'The Kingdom', as they call it down that way. It's a completely different world, exemplified by their love of GAA football and their sheer delight every time the green-and-golds trample the fancy-nancy blue boys from Dublin on their way to yet another All Ireland title. Your Kerry man is a robust, hail-fellow-well-met type full of good cheer and self-belief. I always got the impression that every time he saw me in those early days Seamus mentally ticked off all the major and minor points of Jennifer's previous boyfriends and partners and then sadly came to the conclusion that whatever colour and sass and energy and originality that they had brought to the table, it had all been put into one big pot and boiled down to me, a well-meaning Protestant insurance salesman.

Meanwhile, the brothers, while friendly, could be quite over-bearing, particularly after a few drinks. At first they treated me like some sort of manipulative fiend who had stolen their little princess away from them, until I plumped up the courage one night to remind them that she was no longer sixteen with her hair in bangs. 'She's a mature woman, in her thirties, capable of making her own decisions,' I said. This set them back for a while, particularly the ever-vigilant Kevin, but they never entirely went away, their thinly-veiled jokes about my religion, being so old when I got married and the humdrum of the insurance business remaining always close to the bone. I never really had a balanced, two-way conversation with any of them. Rather, they would hector me into submission, their style of social intercourse based on making a broad, outrageous statement extolling their view on any given topic and ending with an overbearing, 'Are you not agreein' with me now, Stu?' Or, 'I'm telling you, Stu, that's the way it is.'

These statements, generally about how the rest of the world did not live up to their lofty standards, were so breathtaking in their simple-minded, audacious self-belief that finding a quick-fire answer on the spur of the moment was almost impossible. I was always left to mumble a pathetic, 'Yes, probably.' Later, in the quietness of the bathroom, standing before the mirror, I used to curse myself for not having the wherewithal to come up with a snappy reply that would have stopped them in their tracks or at least made them think. Something akin to the content of one of my well constructed Letters To The Editor, but produced there and then, on the spot. Then one day it dawned on me that it would not have mattered what I said because they never listened and they certainly didn't think.

The best thing was to play along with their little game. So I outwardly expressed suitable shock, concern and revulsion when the oldest son, Patrick, was caught having an affair with his marketing manager.

Slinging his clubs into the boot of the car, he had told his wife Kathy that he was off to a weekend business convention in Galway, which would include a round or two of golf. In fact, it was a conference for two, invitation only, and golf was most certainly not on the agenda. He got tripped up when he returned on the Sunday night and Kathy asked him how the golf went, particularly the new putter she had bought him for his birthday only a couple of weeks before. 'Great,' he had replied, 'it worked beautifully. I was rolling them in from a long way out.'

'You certainly were,' she said, producing the putter from the pantry. 'All the feckin' way from here.'

She had taken it out of his bag before he'd left, and as the clubs had stayed in the back of the car all weekend, he had not noticed. His betrayal of his wife and five kids brought his real character to light and after that, while he tried to clean up the mess by perversely seeking a Papal annulment of the marriage, Patrick and his brothers left me pretty much alone.

I can tell you now, when Patrick's world came crashing down, I tut-tutted along with the best of them, and said how terrible it was for the kids. But internally I harboured a great, unbounded shout-it-from-the-roof-tops feeling of unadulterated joy. 'Ha, ha, ha,' I thought, 'Paddy, you smart-arse son of a Kerry man, you got sprung.'

The annulment thing really got to me. How could it be seriously judged that even though five children had been born, the marriage did not exist in the first place?

For me, a marriage should last forever, no matter what. I was determined ours would.

After all, Jennifer was mine; we were a beautiful unit, the complete package.

7

One of the greatest shocks for a newly married man, especially one who has lived the bachelor life until his thirties, is what suddenly happens to his possessions.

Throughout my childhood and adult years, I had never had to share anything with anyone. My toys and sweets and games had been all mine. My books and money and car had been all mine. Even my parents were all mine. I did not have to share them with anyone else either.

When I worked hard, saved my money and finally moved out from Mum and Dad's, the apartment I bought in Dublin was all mine. My name was on the title. Now, so very quickly, it had become 'ours.'

This nettled me a bit. Sure, Jennifer was bringing a property to the marriage. But it was a tiny little terrace in Harold's Cross, stuck right on a busy, grubby main thoroughfare, opposite a 24-hour convenience store that attracted some very unsavoury characters. It was lucky to be half the value of my place, a three bedroom condominium in the heart of Dublin. After a lot of research, I had carefully picked it out and got it at an excellent price because it was a quick-fire 'must-sell' following a messy divorce between the previous yuppie owners. Having saved diligently over the years, I was able to buy it with a substantial deposit and a modest loan. It was almost new, bright and clean, with floor to ceiling windows, plush carpet and plenty of space. I may have fitted it out in typical bachelor style – Jennifer particularly hated the big-screen television slotted in front of the patio doors – but it suited me. It was my place.

The first time I heard Jennifer refer to it as 'our' place was in a conversation over chicken Kiev with two other couples, shortly after we had returned from Bermuda. You know those events, when you're invited to a home dinner party along with another couple you've never met before. Conversation bounces backwards and forwards as the two guest pairings try to work out where the others fit in on the social strata, what they do for a living and what their attitudes are. Heading the list of topics of conversation used to establish these criteria are generally education, the economy and real estate. So, when we got to the subject of property, Jennifer jumped in. 'We're wondering what to do with our place,' she said. 'We think it might be time to sell it and get a house.'

While I was still pondering her use of the word 'our', the husband of the couple we had never met before leapt straight onto this. As it turned out, he was in real estate – well, there you go, then – and had a very clear idea on what to do. 'Sell it, Jennifer,' he enthused. 'Now's the time. You'll get a great price.' And he leaned across to hand her his card, apologising for bringing business to the dinner table but with that smirky shark smile that is the hallmark of the confident realtor.

I got very annoyed with this. 'Hang on,' I thought to myself. 'Isn't this *my* place we are talking about here? Suddenly, it's *our* place! And furthermore, he's ignoring me and talking to Jennifer as if she is the owner and offering her all the advice about flogging it off.'

I was so consumed with this sudden power shift, I stabbed my fork into the chicken Kiev with such force that I squirted hot butter all over the plate and onto the table cloth. 'Bloody hell,' I thought to myself, 'what has Jennifer financially brought into this partnership? Not much in the way of property, that's for sure.' I was about to utter something, a remonstration of some sort, but I thought better of it. What was I going to say? 'Hey, buster, yes, you, the real estate feller, listen, my name's on the title and if you want it, you'll get it from my cold, dead hand?' Hmm. Might put a bit of a dampener on things. Better wait until we get home and talk it over then.

The others continued to prattle on about interest rates, the booming state of the market amid this new, burgeoning Irish economic surge, and the best way to sell the property. They did not take the slightest bit of notice of me as I cleaned up my mess with the neatly-ironed linen napkin. This gave me a little time to calm down and think things through more rationally.

'I guess this is how it will be from now on,' I figured. 'That's what a partnership is all about. And Jennifer is right, of course. We are married, and we now share things. Everything. Our lives, our love, our bodies, our goods, our property. I promised to share everything in the vows we made in the clearing next to the Shannon by the light of the full moon. Mine is hers, and hers is mine. I am hers. And, most importantly, she is mine ...'

I felt a bit more comforted as all this revolved through my mind, and so I took a sip of wine and began to eat the chicken with renewed enthusiasm.

After a minute or so, I was brought back to reality when, out of the corner of my eye, I caught a blinding flash of light. I looked up to see that it was the gleam coming from the pearly white teeth of the real estate shark. He was smiling with enthusiasm, asking me what price would he like me to set on the apartment if we put it on the market right now! A bit taken aback by his cheekiness, I wiped my mouth slowly with my napkin, placed it down carefully on the table in front of me to cover the butter splashes and clasped my hands in front of my face in the shape of a church steeple. I could sense Jennifer getting mightily agitated. I slowly finished swallowing the mouthful of chicken, cleared my throat and said, 'Well, I'm not one to rush into things, but speculatively, I think ninety thousand would be reasonable.' The shark smile grew wider. 'Stuart, the big game is only starting. I can get you another ten, twenty, thirty, fifty grand! No problems. You will be able to buy wherever you want. And pretty soon down the track you'll be able to sell the next one for three times its price if you want. People in the know tell me that the nineties are going to be the biggest boom decade this little country has ever seen.' He leant over and handed me a card. 'Thank you,' I said unruffled, putting it into my jacket pocket. 'I'll, ah, that is, *we* will have a little think about it, won't *we* Jen?' I could feel the daggers from Jennifer's stare piercing the side of my skull.

When we got home, we had our first ever confrontation, of sorts. 'I was just making the point that, in the first instance, this is my house, that's all,' I said calmly. Jennifer turned to go to the bedroom. 'Well, it was yours, and now it's ours,' she said sharply as she headed away from me. 'And soon,' she added, 'it will be sold and we will have a new place!'

This unsettled me. It was a side of her that I had never seen before, a side I did not like. I followed her into the bedroom and as I walked past her to go to the en suite, I lifted her chin and lightly slapped her face and said to her quietly but firmly, 'Just be careful what you say, darling,' and left it at that. She looked at me, put her hand to her cheek, and went very quiet. I had never been one to fire back at people, but this time I did. And it felt good. I felt I had scored a little victory.

As it turned out, shark's teeth was as good as his word. Rather than the more traditional style of a private sale, he took the apartment to auction against my better judgment, danced across the stage in front of the crowd like Mick Jagger, used my compliant father as a dummy bidder to up the ante – a bottle of Jameson's insured his inspired participation – and came up with an extra thirty-seven thousand five hundred. It was an astonishing result, giving us the opportunity to buy a home in, of all places, Dalkey. Bang, we were suddenly living harbour-side in Dublin's dress circle, in a location many people would have died for. Dalkey is a beautiful suburb, right on the water, south of the port of Dun Laoghaire, and I detected just a little tinge of surprise bordering on envy from friends when we told them where we had bought. 'Feckin' hell, Stu,' said Buchanan when I told him. 'You'll be working your arse off to pay for that.'

Of course, it was good old shark's teeth who not only found the Dalkey home for us, but who also sold Jennifer's little pad, thus providing him with a bonanza in commissions. As the three of us stood out on the front lawn with the smell of the Irish Sea in our nostrils, I reckon his smile could have been seen from Liverpool. He must have loved to see strangers like me wander into a mutual friend's place for a chicken Kiev.

But I will admit, despite my original misgivings about what was 'hers' and what was 'mine', Jennifer and the real estate whiz-kid had been right in their determinaton to get things under way quickly. The day we moved into the house was for me almost as exciting as the day of our wedding. Our new home had charm, space, light, warmth and a beautiful family feel about it. It had only two bedrooms but there was opportunity to expand, plus a large, well-equipped kitchen and a lounge room that could almost have accommodated my old apartment. Sorry, 'our' old apartment.

In retrospect, I guess it was good that that this small but significant discussion about selling my place had happened in front of other people. I often reflect what I might have said to Jennifer if she had first used the expression 'our place' to me without someone else in the room. Say, across the breakfast table on a Monday morning as we were both heading out to work. Would I have got upset and fired back: 'What do you mean our place?', leading us into a heated discussion and onto God knows where. The whole thing could have blown up there and then.

No, she was right, and things were going to be fine. I may have lost sole ownership of an apartment, but I had gained a whole new beautiful home and a delightful wife to manage it. Now, that was a real possession. Something to be proud of. And to never let go, under any circumstances.

8

Then, we slipped into second gear. I don't mean that in a negative or derogatory sense. I sometimes think second gear is a beautiful place to be in, providing of course we are talking about an original, classic three-speed gear-box, and not one of those hi-tech six-level electronic systems they use these days. Second gear is more productive and pacey than first and has a touch of acceleration about it. A sense of going somewhere, with the additional element of a slight roaring sound to add to the excitement. But it is not as exhilarating as third, and therefore not as dangerous. In second, despite its limitations, you are able to get anywhere and achieve what you want without going over the top.

Cruising along in second gear at home meant I was travelling nicely at work. I would go off each morning, proud of myself and my beautiful wife and our wonderful house, and concentrate on the job at hand all day.

While I was a part-owner of the business, along with Derek, I saw my role as a vertical one, handling a wide range of tasks from managerial at the top right down to sales. That's just the way I am in life, really. I like to be involved in everything. Sure, I trusted my staff, but I wanted to ensure that they maintained the standards that I thought were appropriate. I kept up selling, so as not to get stale. I loved sales. A sale of a new policy was always a delight for me, the presentation of a new product to the staff was a joy, and examining our constantly growing turnover figures provided me with a feeling of immense satisfaction. Even outlining policies to potential clients who I knew from experience were not going to sign on was an engaging challenge. I loved to walk them through the detail of the benefits, the bonuses, the premiums, the payment options. The art was to try and keep my enthusiasm on an even keel. Not get too pushy and come across as a salesman but hold back – drop into second gear – and become their confidante, advisor and friend, outlining to them how, at the end of the day, this was going to be good for them. I truly believed it and wanted my clients to appreciate that, too.

Not only that, I could see big things happening in Ireland. The economy, as our shark's teeth real estate man had predicted, was beginning to really boom and I had in the back of my mind that Derek and I could move the business even further into financial services – advice, brokering, property investment, that sort of thing. I was in a happy place.

But then, not long after we had moved to Dalkey, Jennifer started talking about having a baby! This came as a big jolt, right out of the blue. It was all a bit too fast for me. I would have preferred to have waited a little longer and enjoyed our time as newlyweds, appreciating the world and our new home together like two young lovers rather than being catapulted into the disciplined domain of parenthood. I wanted to be able to take my beautiful wife out and, I will admit, show her off to the world. I will make no bones about it. Consider what had happened so far. By my early thirties, I looked like I was going to be a solitary man forever, sitting in my sparsely furnished Dublin flat all by myself, making two minute pasta, watching the *Late Late Show* and reading biographies about Bill Gates, Bill Cullen and Alan Sugar. Then suddenly, I had this vivacious woman at my side, a person that even the harshest critic would describe as a great catch, lighting up any room she walked into. Why shouldn't I want to show her off?

One of the great advantages was that Jennifer was brilliant with all people at all levels. While I had certain comunicative skills, particularly in a business setting, I always found events such as parties a challenge. Removed from my comfortable platform of the sales spiel, I found myself either standing in a corner with a warm drink or being the silent one amongst the group as all the others told heroic tales or comical stories. With Jennifer, it was different. She captivated everyone around her, but all the while she couldn't wait to get home so that we could make love. No, wait, let me re-phrase that. So that we could have sex.

Now, I was not the greatest lover, I will admit that. I had not had a lot of experience, and I know that my first few clumsy attempts in the early days of our relationship were pretty rapid fire. I just couldn't help myself, climaxing very quickly, and I appreciated Jennifer's patience and forebearance. But even I knew that within a few short weeks of our wedding we had left the realms of intimacy and had lurched into the world of mechanics. Spontaneity was replaced by a strict regime centred around the calendar. 'Hear that?' she would say, cupping her hand to her ear theatrically. 'That's the sound of my biological clock ticking.'

'Yes, darling, I hear it.'

'It's five minutes to midnight and they're playing the last waltz, Fred Astaire. You'd better get your dancing shoes on.'

I loved her and was proud of her, but I was not yet ready to share her with children. Nevertheless, pregnancy became our number one target. And that, in Jennifer's mind, could only be achieved by total adherence to her carefully plotted strategy. It was high pressure and intensely technical. Phrases such as 'predicting ovulation' and 'cervical mucous' and 'basal body temperature' became part of our daily lexicon. Trouble was, despite the highly-scheduled logistics and our combined physical efforts, the system had a hidden malfunction somewhere. No matter when, where or how often we rigidly stuck to the cycle, nothing would eventuate.

Jennifer would disappear into the en suite with the pregnancy tester and I would hear her ripping the cover off it and having a wee, followed by the slap of the toilet lid as she would sit down and wait for the result. Then, after what would seem to be an interminable time, she would come out. The first few times she was disappointed but not defeated. Then over the course of the next few months there came expressions of despondency, frustration, anger, and finally the phrase I was silently anticipating. 'You,' she shouted after many months, waving the negative result at me. 'It must be your fault! You're firing blanks, you big useless bollocks.'

Maybe I was. That thought had regularly crossed my mind. I was getting older and had never fathered a child. I was from a family that were not big breeders, our miniscule attendance at the wedding attesting to that. I was not what you would call a sexual dynamo, a rumpy-pumpy master of the good Rogering, a Barry White love god. Far from it. It could well be that the fault was mine.

There was only one way to find out.

Under her instructions, I obediently made an appointment with a men's health clinic in Sandyford, and dutifully turned up at the spartan, ultra-clean office. The nurse gave me a small bottle and directed me to a little cubicle, inside of which there was a chair, a table and the only other accoutrement, a pile of well-thumbed men's magazines, amongst which I discovered a copy of *Penthouse*. After scrutinising the picture spread of that edition's centre-fold, a slithery brunette named Krista, followed by some rather embarrassing one-handed action, I filled the bottle to the half way point, tidied myself up, and offered both it and the *Penthouse* back to the nurse. She took the bottle and applied a sticker to it. 'You can put the magazine back in the room,' she said icily.

A few days later the specialist, a cheery, Scots fellow with rosy cheeks and flourishing ginger sideboards, slapped me on the shoulder, leaned close and said, 'Laddie, ye've got enough wee wriggly fellers in that bottle to impregnate an entire Highland village.' Praise the Lord, the test had proved Jennifer wrong! I still had plenty left in the tank. I walked out of his office beaming, only to disappear unsmiling into the desperate world of IVF.

Look, it all sounds very well. 'We'll take an egg from you, Jennifer, and some sperm from you, Stuart, mix them in a Petri dish, say a few magic words while waving our hands over the top, put it all back inside and Bob's your uncle.' At least, that was how it seemed to be presented to me. But, my God, it was difficult. It was a painful experience for Jennifer, her body being pushed and probed and bullied into submission. 'Harvested' was one term they used, which made my blood boil. It sounded like my wife, my beautiful wife, was some sort of field or tree from which they were going to reap grain or fruit. The physical agony was only matched by the emotional stress as each failure confirmed in Jennifer's mind that the minute hand on her famous clock was edging rapidly closer to midnight. The last waltz was almost over and I could feel the soles on my dancing pumps wearing perilously thin.

And then one day, miracle of miracles, things 'took' and suddenly our first little baby was on the way. I can't tell you how powerful was the sense of relief and joy that swept through us both. I was walking on water and, better still, the furrowed, angst-ridden look that had begun to blight Jennifer's pretty face disappeared. If she looked beautiful the night I married her, then she absolutely blossomed through that first pregnancy. Morning sickness, the emotional see-saw, concerns about the health of the baby, they certainly came and went, but she overrode them all with a mixture of happiness and determination. The sense of achievement drove her on, and I thought to myself, 'You know, this is what she really wants.' And when a little boy arrived on a cold Dublin morning all pink and squishy, with a slight bruise on his forehead but otherwise perfectly healthy, we just held him and thought, 'Haven't we done well?'

Funny thing is, the next two babies – another little boy and then, seven years later, a daughter for Jennifer – came without any IVF help at all. Anything can happen when you relax. Especially if you drop back into second gear.

9

I think I was a pretty good father. An absent one maybe, perhaps at crucial moments when I might have been of greater assistance at home, but overall still pretty good.

I didn't get much guidance from my family in the art of engaging with children. For my father, the ever mobile military man, the way of launching conversation with me as a child was to ask, 'Geared up and ready for battle, Stuart?' And in terms of being parents themselves, Jennifer's father and her four brothers weren't particularly good role models either, especially Patrick, who sabotaged his whole family unit for the sake of a bit of sex on the side.

So while the world was rapidly changing around me and the New Age Dad was becoming de rigueur, I tended to adopt the old-fashioned view that I was the father and the bread winner and Jennifer was the mother and the family manager. Well, from my reading, that technique had worked successfully for centuries, so why fix it when it was not broken? Sure, I pitched in and did things more than my Dad and those of his generation did. I was not an entirely silent, non-existent father. I loved to play with the kids in the evening and made a point of being with them as much of the weekend as I could, depending on golf commitments or judo lessons. But after two other fruitless careers, I knew insurance was my game, my opportunity for success, and it was important to me that I concentrated hard on that and made the best of it in order to benefit everyone. I saw myself as the provider of the family, the tribal head, the hunter, the gatherer. And in that situation, what the chief says, goes.

So there I was, a bachelor in my late thirties, a three-time Dad in my fifties. I read books with the kids and played hide-and-seek around the garden and held their tiny hands as we strolled around the port at Dun Laoghaire. I loved taking them down to Bulloch Harbour, which was not far from us, just past the Martello Tower.

We would wait patiently on the edge of the slippery blue-stone pier for the appearance of a pair of seals that had taken up habitation around there. The kids were always thrilled when the two large, black, quizzically humorous faces would suddenly break the water with a rushing, whooshing sound. This maritime odd couple would then stare at us with a look along the lines of, 'So, what are you doing here, then?' It was very hard to obey the signs not to feed them, but it was worth it, because we got to know the scene and the people down there very well. One of the perks was being able to order a nice fresh lobster for dinner. I always loved this part because although Jennifer was vegetarian, she considered fresh fish, particularly lobster, as not being too far out of her strict regimen and the meal we would have that night would be delicious.

I know I was a solid, conservative type but generally speaking, particularly in the early days, I would let the kids tease and manipulate me and I would take it all in good stead and come back for more. Within reason, of course. I would kick the rugby ball with the boys and help them with their hurling and soccer. I showed them some of the finer points of judo, particularly for their own self-defence, with a view to them perhaps taking it up. There was one time that Jennifer bought them a kite for Christmas and we had a great time putting it together and taking it to a local park on a windy day. After a few failed lift-offs and some serious nose-into-the-turf crashes, we finally got it off the ground and it flew beautifully like a bird until young Richard managed to loop it over some power wires and we went home empty-handed.

The boys and I also worked in the garden together, turning the sandy soil over and planting little rows of flowers such as nasturtiums and clusters of veggies, including potatoes and carrots. Some grew well, and a lot didn't, but none through lack of trying. I was very insistent that the boys helped me with this task. I saw it as a great model of what life was all about; that is, you get out what you put in. 'If you select the right seeds, plant them at the right time, cultivate them carefully and tend the plot, you will get a good result,' I would say to them. 'But if you do it in a slapdash way, you will get very little in return.'

There were great moments of celebration in the kitchen when the boys would proudly and triumphantly bring in some of their fresh produce for Jennifer to cook for dinner. But if they were tardy and weeds started to spring up, I would make it clear to them that they were not being responsible and that I was unhappy with their performance. Jennifer used to complain sometimes that I was getting on their backs about this too much but I felt that she was entirely wrong on this matter.

'As you sow, so you shall reap,' I would say to her. 'It's in the good book.'

'Which good book is that, darling?' she said to me one day. 'The Bible? Or the insurer's handbook?'

Despite her taunts or criticism, no one could take any of those fatherly moments away from me. But if the situation came down to deciding between spending the time at the office working on something important rather than being at home, then I felt that for the good of the family work and career came first. We had a beautiful house in an exclusive address with three lovely children, and with us both agreeing that Jennifer would stay at home and run it, someone had to pay the bills. That was me. And I was proud to do it.

Fatherhood is a challenging task, an extremely tricky business, particularly developing an enduring relationship with each of your children as they come along. My approach, despite my Protestant background, was to adopt the Jesuit philosophy: 'Give me a child until he is seven, and I will give you the man.' That is, I would begin with a clean slate and shape him or her into my own self image in those first impressionable years.

Buchanan, whose children were older than ours, thought I was crazy. 'Jayzus, Stu,' he said, 'they come out of that womb stamped with their own personality. They're hard-wired. You're taking on a big challenge if you reckon you can re-configure the little feckers to suit you.'

Well, I was up for it and as it turned out our first born, Stuart Junior, was well-named because he was a replica of me. Friends, family and sometimes even perfect strangers pointed to the similarity wherever we went. 'You'll never be dead while that one is around,' they would say, a rather gruesome sort of praise I always thought. He not only had my blocky shape and the dark hair I once had, but a lot of my mannerisms as well. He was thoughtful, reserved and calculating. He never rushed into things, preferring to weigh up all the consequences first before deciding on a course of action, whether that was stacking a pile of building blocks together or learning to ride a bike. He was the delight of my life. We kicked the soccer ball, threw rugby passes to each other, played Transformers and wrestled on the grass.

Initially I thought he was going to be a bit shy like I was and Jennifer and I worked hard at trying to draw him out – me because I had been through all that before and knew how crushing it could be and Jennifer because, as she used to say, 'Shyness is not part of my family's make-up.'

He blossomed into an engaging child, bordering almost on cheeky. He took great joy in ordering his little brother around and teasing his little sister and speaking up with confidence amongst friends, family and school mates.

Our second boy, Richard, was a different kettle of fish. He was the thoughtful, poetic type, more contemplative and arty rather than physical. Sure, he played games with me and Junior but he would pack it in if things got a bit rough. He would hang around the kitchen a bit too much for my liking, listening in on every bit of gossip that passed between Jenny and her family and friends. He knew everything that was going on around the place. Jennifer said it was because he had her sense of spirituality and was showing something called his 'feminine side', which quite frankly worried the hell out of me. In my opinion, that sounded like the first step down the path to homosexuality and I certainly did not want that to happen to either of my boys. I worked particularly hard on him to toughen him up.

After intense discussion, we had named him after my father – and me, too, seeing as Richard is my second name. Jennifer was not too happy about this, as she wanted to honor her Dad. I never actually laid it on the line, but I think she knew that while I appreciated Seamus as my father-in-law and would never speak ill of him publicly, privately I considered him a rogue. A loveable rogue, but one you could never really trust, and trust to me is one of the most important foundations of life. He was a larger-than-life, flight-of-fancy man with a loud voice, a thumping slap on the back, a love of a drink and an innate ability to win or lose vast amounts of money on the turn of a card or a photo finish at the Leopardstown races. He had a beautiful home in Blackrock and there always seemed to be plenty of cash around, but the path he had followed to achieve such a comfortable existence had been pretty rocky.

In the years since he had left his beloved County Kerry as a young man to seek his fortune, he had worked in an abattoir, dug ditches and driven lorries. Then he realised he needed to get into business for himself. From that point on he had variously bought and sold property, been in the motor trade, wholesaled fish, ran a fleet of hot dog vans and imported laptops, despite being totally clueless about computers. He could read the shift in the market beautifully, successfully developing a string of bouncing castle franchisees, having realised early on that that particular amusement was becoming a very important part of every Irish First Communion home party. Recognizing Ireland was becoming an island of ageing, creaking knees struggling to get up after genuflecting, he flooded the health food market with dubious fish oil capsules imported from God knows where, making a packet before the authorities shut it down.

Setbacks like that never stifled him and he would bounce back with his characteristic grin. If there was a quid in it, Seamus Fitzgerald O'Brien was prepared to have a go at it, no matter what the risk. Likeable rogue that he was, I did not want my son to be named after someone like that. So I came up with a compromise.

'You can use Seamus for a name if we have a third boy,' I promised Jennifer.

Of course, there were no more boys. But there was a little girl born much later and so when I suggested that she be called Moira after my mother, Jennifer was shocked. 'You said that I could name the next one after Dad,' she said. I replied that that was true, but seeing as this was a girl and not a boy then that had changed things. 'If we follow the theme of having used my name first and then Dad's name,' I said, 'then it is logical to name this little one after Mum.'

Jennifer wanted to name the little girl Mary after her own mother. 'That just doesn't fit,' I said. 'It ruins the sequence.' There was a moody silence in the house for several days over this issue, one that we both felt very strongly about. Eventually, she came back with a new suggestion. 'All right, if you insist on your method, let's make it a version of Mary,' she said. 'Let's call her Molly.'

Molly! I really didn't like that name. It sounded old fashioned, bog Irish and a bit common. It reminded me of that folk song about Molly Malone, the 'tart with the cart', selling shellfish in the Dublin streets, a business that I did not consider all that attractive although Seamus would have been in it like a shot if he had thought there was money to be made. I didn't want my daughter linked with that sort of image. I tried to push for something else but realised that in her post-birth state this was upsetting Jennifer very much and the house was losing its calm, tranquil atmosphere that I insisted on. So after quietly doing some more research on names, I came downstairs one morning and grandly said, 'Okay, Molly it is.'

You could see the look of relief in Jennifer's eyes and within a matter of minutes the birth registration form had been filled out. 'Thank you, darling,' she said. 'I'm glad you could see my view.'

'Oh, I'm happy, too,' I said. 'You know how you said that Molly is a derivation of Mary? Well, so is Moira, Mum's name …'

She set her jaw firmly and marched out of the room and on that day the lines were set without another word being spoken – the boys would be 'mine' and Molly would be 'hers'. In an unwritten contract, I could take the boys wherever I wanted to, shape them into whatever I liked, and plan their whole lives without Jennifer's interference. In turn, the little girl could be hers to, as I used to say, 'Molly-coddle as much as you like.' I thought the play on words was pretty clever.

Stuart Junior developed my acumen for figures and I was sure he would go into something along the same lines as I did. I often entertained the thought that after he had been to university he could join me at the business and work his way up and ultimately take it over when it was time for me to retire. As for Richard, I figured that if I worked hard enough with him I would soon de-tune some of his arty-farty influences and toughen him up to take on life's experiences like a real man.

And Molly? Well, I always felt that with her anything could happen. She was certainly her mother's daughter. The same red hair, green eyes and palest of skin, mixed with the same flighty approach to life. We used to play a little game where I would pick her up and pretend to drop her, and then catch her just as it appeared she was going to hit the ground. Sometimes I would start the game with her high up around my shoulders. Other times I would hold her out flat in my arms, as if I was making an offering to the gods, and let her go. I got very good at releasing her and then catching her at the very, very last second, which only added to the thrill and the enjoyment. My judo training helped me a lot with my reflexes but so did the fact that she was such a tiny little thing, always small for her age. 'Catch-Molly game, Daddy?' she would say. And, 'Catch-Molly again,' when she begged for more. Jennifer would just look away. 'Someone's going to get hurt,' she would mutter. 'It will all end in tears.'

One day, I caught her at the very last second, the back of her head just touching the ground and she looked up at me and I froze. The melancholy image of the little girl with the sad green eyes in the painting on the wall of our wedding night suite in the Roscommon manor suddenly came back to me, unsettling me for days.

But our little game aside, I knew that Molly was Jennifer's girl, her precious jewel. They held confidences between themselves, laughed at each other's quaint jokes and could almost read each other's minds. This concerned me. I felt excluded from their close-knit little club. I wanted some influence over her, because I didn't want her to grow up to be as frivolous as Jennifer. I often think that the development of this cosy little relationship irritated me so much that other aspects of Jennifer's approach to life started to get under my skin.

The constant chatter with everyone around her, especially her extended family, started to really grate.

When we were over at the Blackrock family home she and her mother and her aunties would talk for hours and then, just when I thought we were going to leave and I could go home, pour a drink and relax in front of the television, one of them would say something like, 'Oh, did you hear Aoifa, you know, Sean's wife, is going to have a baby?' And someone would say, 'No way, never!' And it would start all over again and we would be there for another twenty frustrating minutes.

'Who the hell is Aoifa?' I used to think to myself. 'And who gives a damn?'

But the big change between me and Jennifer was this: once Molly was born, pretty much all love-making, which had been a reasonable part of our lives, if only as a means to an end, went out the window. I found this so frustrating especially as I had been what I considered to be a noble and honourable participant in our 'trying-to-make-babies' period, including the rather unsavoury experience of masturbating over a pornographic magazine in a little cubicle, and now I had been hung out to dry. This annoyed me. Particularly in the context of Jennifer's Buddhist beliefs. Where was all the peace, love, harmony and ringing of bells now? Weren't Buddhists supposed to be sharing, caring types? Make love, not war? They certainly talked up all that airy-fairy nonsense about spirituality and the after-life, but when it came to the practical exercising of that option, they were sadly lacking. To rub salt into the wound, she would be on the phone for hours spreading the gospel of love among her circle of like-minded friends, especially Wendy, her little pal from New Zealand, and Karena who was some sort of guru. I said to Jennifer one day, 'You talk about the notion of love, you promote the concept of love, but you don't actually make love. Certainly not with me.'

So I fell in love with someone else.

10

Was it love? It was probably lust. Whatever it was, it came about when my business partner Derek had to pull out of an international insurance conference at the last minute. 'Something's come up, Stuart,' he said. 'I have to stay in Dublin. You go instead.'

Being Stuart the reliable workhorse, I replied that flattered as I was, I could do no such thing. 'I have a pile of work on my plate a mile high and three very good leads that I'm certain can be converted into sales,' I said. But Derek was insistent. 'Go on, lad. You deserve it. And it won't be all work out there. Buchanan's going, too, so the craic will be great. And they say Dubrovnik is beautiful.'

I had never been there before. Having three kids, Jennifer and I used to opt for the family holiday in the Mediterranean each year. Usually Spain, sometimes Portugal. Having travelled to all sorts of places in all sorts of ways, she was happy to spend her vacation in an apartment by a beach. Sometimes as an alternative we camped, hiking through the hills and enjoying the beautiful crags and dales of Ireland and Scotland.

But Dubrovnik? It was a whole world away. A lot of travel for who knows what? Nevertheless, Derek assured me that if the three potential sales did come good he would ensure I got a suitable whack out of them. So whether I liked it or not, I was off to Croatia.

Looking through the schedule with Jennifer before I flew out, I figured it was going to be a hectic experience. Seven days of seminars, speeches and workshops on the theme of 'Insurance, Through The Looking Glass.' Now, despite my devotion to the industry, and there were not too many who approached it with the level of enthusiasm that I did, even I conceded that with a title like that it was going to be pretty dull. But I, along with the four hundred and thirty-five others who gathered from around the world, had not counted on the presence of Federica.

Federica Baumgartner was the keynote speaker for the conference. She was Swiss, tall and slim, with perfect white skin and long dark hair which she kept tied up in a bun. Her blue eyes, showing a clarity and intelligence that was almost frightening, assessed you calmly through a most impressive set of designer glasses. Her trim, athletic figure, chiselled no doubt through many hours in the gym, was accentuated by beautifully cut business suits matched with crisp white shirts and discreet although obviously very expensive ear-rings.

And did she know her stuff! Not only she had studied business in her own country, she had topped it off with a Masters at Harvard and then had gone on to rise through the ranks of a Californian electronics firm to the position of vice-president. She had apparently cut a swathe as she went, dragging it out of potential bankruptcy and putting it back on top before the glass ceiling stymied her from getting the top job. By the time she came into our orbit she had spent the previous five years travelling the world as a consultant, resuscitating flagging companies and speaking at seminars like ours.

As well as the main address, her contract also required her to stay for the week, sitting in on workshops and offering individual advice. How lucky were we? She strode briskly around the hotel like a Swiss goddess who had come down from the snow-topped mountains to save us. Even if she was out of sight, you knew she was approaching because of the click-clack of the Prada heels on the floor, the surge of energy that whooshed into the room and the subtle but sensuous aroma of her perfume. 'It's Bulgari Black,' an American women delegate whispered to me once as she floated past. 'Bergamot, vanilla and sandalwood. Very hip.'

Initially, I felt that it wasn't so much her looks that got people in, but what she said. Her opening speech was exhilarating, a powerful rally cry that dragged us out of our lethargy and had us primed to run through brick walls. Her performances in the smaller study groups and workshops were simply amazing. She didn't hector us from the lectern but sat amongst us, pushing us for concepts and solutions, preferring chunks of crayon on white paper to thrash out things rather than asphyxiating death by PowerPoint. She had terrific ideas to throw into the mix and get us started. If she came to your desk, she would grab a chair and sit beside you, hitting you at eye level, looking at your work, encouraging you to push forward. Her passion for achievement was overwhelming, the ideas she threw up liberating and the challenges she gave us a genuine buzz. I have never seen people in the insurance game so excited about their products, their potential and their future. And believe me, that is saying something.

Of course, a handful of the older, burnt-out types thought it was a load of bollocks while some of the younger brigade considered it an interesting but minor irritant before the lunch-time lager, having taken a liking to the local brew, Velebitsko. But most of us thought it was riveting. Especially me. That was because, while I understood and tolerated Jennifer's pre-occupation with Buddhism and her zeal for all things New Age, to me that was a lot of beads-and-incense mumbo-jumbo. Airy-fairy stuff about finding yourself, sitting in ashrams and getting in accord with the positive vibe. I accept that we were married by the light of the moon in a clearing next to a river during the summer solstice, and externally I gave the impression that I was supportive of the general philosophy, but quite frankly a lot of that stuff failed to grab me. Jennifer might have had a bit of success before we met with her little books about finding 'the inner you', and I regularly acknowledged her for it. The point was, they were really a fine example of marketing genius, somehow persuading people to buy sixty pages of homilies, believing that they were going to change their lives for good forever. In the real world, in the one-on-one, down-to-earth, let's-sign-the-contract-now business world, that sort of touchy-feely nonsense gets you nowhere.

Federica, on the other hand, had a powerful, straight-forward, believable message. An inspiring message. A realistic message. Not setting loony goals but achievable targets, working towards them, getting them done, then moving on to the next ones.

The thing was, she made me realise that I was a well-meaning, moderately-successful type that was a bit too stodgy, and who was simply digging the trench longer and deeper. Now, here she was talking about getting out of the trench, criss-crossing the field, digging fresh holes, finding new opportunities, creating new concepts.

'Above all,' she said, 'be an individual, be selfish, don't be ashamed, do it for yourself first! Then your business and your family can share in the success that will naturally follow. The world is there for your taking. Grab what you want, use it up and when you are finished with it, spit it out.'

Very quickly I began falling in love with her presentation skills. Rather rapidly I began falling in love with her ideas. Pretty soon I found myself falling in love with her.

Of course, I told myself, it was only a fleeting thought, a moment of lunacy, something that would surely never materialise. And then it happened. After sitting in on a workshop where I stood up and contributed a few words about the importance of remaining loyal to your clients, Federica discreetly sidled up to me at the morning coffee break. 'Hmm,' she said, 'Stuart, I see you're still in second gear …'

Well, this floored me. Second gear! This was my own personal philosophy, something I had pursued successfully most of my life, particularly during our marriage. But it was a description that I had never mentioned to anyone, ever! Not even Jennifer.

'Second gear? How did you ..?' That was all I could utter, stumbling for words as the coffee cup in my hand began to shake. Federica looked straight at me with her steel blue eyes. 'Oh, I've been watching you,' she said. 'Don't worry, Stuart Hoare, it's part of my role. To observe all around me, see who is doing what, and decide where I can encourage talent.'

'Um, you've read me like a book,' I blurted.

She looked around the room and then leaned close to me. For the first time she was not speaking in her power voice or causing heads to turn. She was softer, more personal, very private. 'I can see a more capable, more effective person trying to get out, Stuart,' she whispered. She waited calmly for a few seconds and then went on. 'You have certain skills and a genuine desire to achieve. You are a nice man. But hidden underneath I can see a stronger man, a more in-control man, a man who could produce even better results. A real Celtic Tiger! I can help that man emerge.'

She touched my arm. My cup shook some more. She leaned closer to me. The aroma of the Bulgari Black was enchanting. If I had never smelt the combination of bergamot, vanilla and sandalwood before, I was certainly getting a nose full of it now.

'You can do a lot more in top gear, Stuart,' she whispered. She touched me once more on the arm, smiled, turned and left.

What happened after that? Well, I think it is called something like cabin fever or seminar syndrome, or some such. A couple rapidly developing an emotional link within the exciting, surreal and temporary environment of a conference. Isolated from the humdrum of their jobs, removed from the tedium of domestic life and charged up by the freedom, the food and the drink, they let themselves go. They find someone they can relate to, a person they can discuss different ideas with, a neutral associate they can pour their heart out to. And while it begins on a professional level, then a friendly one, then an emotional one, it can rapidly lurch into a physical one.

I was beginning to think, 'Why not? Jennifer and I rarely make love anymore and when we do, it's pretty perfunctory.'

Before I knew it, into the third day, Federica with her power, precision and vision had intrigued me, engaged me and finally besotted me. It's impossible to describe how it can happen in such a short amount of time but it did. We began sitting next to each other at every possible opportunity, including all meals. I would attend all her seminars and at the end of each we would head off and have a drink. In the evenings, we would go out into the Old Town of Dubrovnik, marvelling at the people, the art, the buildings, the restaurants, the entertainers.

It wasn't long before I found myself in her room. We had had dinner, it was late, and now we were quaffing drinks from the mini-bar; cognac for her, whiskey for me. It was great to share a real drink with someone instead of the usual situation where I would be the only one having alcohol while Jennifer would be somehow getting enjoyment out of a glass of exotic fruit juices topped up with wheatgrass. I knew I was in dangerous territory but, what the heck, I couldn't help it, could I? Federica kicked off her shoes, tossed her glasses onto the sideboard and pulled the comb out of her long dark hair, letting it cascade down to her shoulders. Up until this point, she had been business beautiful, now she was simply stunning. She began to slowly open the top button of her crisp white shirt. I thought to myself, 'Stuart, it's now or never, top gear or nothing. Perhaps even over-drive.'

But the brandy was having an effect and she was becoming less focused and letting her normally impenetrable guard down. She continued to talk. And talk, and talk and talk. As she went on, it suddenly dawned on me that over our time together we had chatted only very occasionally about me, my family, my job and my marriage. While she had forecast that she was going to draw out the hidden, inner me, ninety five per cent of the time the conversation had been focused entirely on Federica. About her background, her education, her career, her time at the electronics firm, her achievements, her fights with the board, her resignation, the growth of her consultancy, her ups, her downs, her defeats, her successes. I think there was some mention of a husband in there, now long gone, but I can't be sure. 'Poor bastard,' I thought, 'he probably died of boredom.'

I stared into my whiskey as the voice droned on, suddenly reining myself back into the present just in time to hear her say, 'But for all my achievements, Stuart, I am lonely. Very, very lonely. If you know what I mean.'

I knew what this meant. You'd have to be daft not to. I was about to say, 'And I think I know why.' But I thought the better of it and just stared straight at her.

'What?' she said, surprised. For the first time since things had warmed up between us, I had not replied like a lapdog. 'Didn't you hear me?' she asked.

'Er, yes, yes,' I replied. 'You're lonely, and that's not good. Excuse me, I have to go to the toilet.'

She looked puzzled and a little miffed as I stood up and headed through the door to the spectacular glass and marble bathroom. I flipped up the lid and had a pee, trying to regroup my thoughts and work out what to do next. One voice in my head, smooth, controlled, seductive, began telling me to take direct action. 'Go on, Stuart,' it crooned, 'be a man, get into top gear! Go back in there and screw her brains out. She's begging for a good old-fashioned shag and you're the man to do it.' Then another voice, anxious, almost hysterical, began calling for a halt. 'Stuart!' it hissed, 'you're a married man! You can't be unfaithful, no matter how bad you think things are at home.'

As I stood at the sink washing my hands and staring into the mirror, with both voices fighting for victory across the battleground of my confused brain, the buzz on my mobile suddenly went off, indicating a message had come through. I dried my hands, pulled the phone out of my pocket and called it up. The message loomed into view. It was a picture Jennifer had sent of the kids. The three of them were all in their pyjamas and dressing gowns, ready for bed. 'Goodnight, Daddy,' the caption read. 'We love you.'

I stared at the picture and message for a long time, then looked at myself in the mirror and swore. I was shocked at what I saw staring back at me. My days and nights carousing with Federica had extracted a heavy toll. My eyes were bloodshot, they had bags under them, and my skin was flushed. I looked like Patrick did after he had been sprung. Washed up and ready to roll down the road into deserved oblivion. 'God,' I thought, 'he lost everything. Am I going to do the same?'

I took one more look at the photo, read the caption again, closed the phone and put it back in my pocket. I sprinkled some water on my face, dried it, tidied my clothes, slicked my hair back with my hands and took a deep breath and mumbled the burning question to myself. 'So, what's it to be? Fuck, or flee?'

I opened the bathroom door. There she was, already lying in the bed, covered only by a sheet. In a direct change to her usual orderly way of doing things, her clothes, including her expensive white satin bra and knickers, were flung all over the floor.

'Come on, Stuart,' Federica cooed, crooking her finger at me, 'time to get into top gear.' Without taking her eyes off me, she threw back the sheet to reveal her trim, fit body. The startling whiteness of her skin highlighted the blackness of her long flowing locks and the pinkness of her nipples. My eyes darted down to see how her pubic hair would stand out against this dramatic background, but perhaps not surprisingly, it had been waxed and shaved down to the barest vertical tuft with typical Swiss precision. My God, she was beautiful. That first little voice that had spoken to me, the evil one, was certainly on the money. She was ready for it and I was the man to deliver.

As she lay there on her side, gesturing me to come over, I put my hand out towards her. And then I suddenly pulled it away and put it to my forehead. It was the other voice, the good voice, coming on strong in my brain. 'Don't, Stuart,' it was whispering. 'Don't do this! You'll lose your marriage, your family, your business …'

My head jolted backwards. That was the clincher. I looked at Federica, put both hands up, palms out, and whispered, 'No.'

'What?' she said, incredulous.

'No,' I said. 'No. I can't. You're beautiful, Federica, an amazing woman, and I think I'm in love with you, but …' My voice trailed off and I began to head for the door. She pounced off the bed to try and stop me, shouting, 'What? What are you doing? Stuart, I thought that we had something …?' She might have been fit, she might have been fast, she might have looked absolutely gorgeous rushing at me with her pert little breasts leading the charge, but the brandy had dulled her reflexes enough for me to grab the advantage. I got to the handle first, swung the door open and stepped quickly out into the corridor. She followed me out and stood there, unashamedly naked, her voice ringing in my ears as I strode determinedly away, not looking back. 'You weak little man, Stuart,' she shouted. 'You will amount to nothing!

Fucking nothing!' Her voice echoed down the corridor. Then the door slammed. I could hear other doors discreetly opening, wary guests investigating what the noise was all about, as I scurried down the hallway towards the elevator.

Next morning, I had breakfast in my room; I attended none of her sessions for the rest of the day; I avoided her at all costs for the remainder of the conference. Our paths crossed just once, during a coffee break, and she simply stared right through me, shrugged and said, 'Ha!'

On the final morning, as we assembled in reception to catch the bus for the airport, I noticed Buchanan walking past in his swimming gear, towel draped over his shoulder, heading for the pool. I stopped him. 'What on earth are you doing?' I said. 'Aren't you on the same flight home as me?'

He grinned widely. 'I'm staying on for a day or two,' he said.

I stepped back, confused. 'What about the family?'

'Family?' he said. 'Stuart, they don't understand me. Nuala's on my back all the time and the kids just play computer games. My only friends are the goldfish and the dog. I'm better off here.'

He glanced over my shoulder at someone obviously standing some distance behind me and his smile grew broader. I didn't need to turn around. I knew who it was. The smell of bergamot, vanilla and sandalwood floating through reception was undeniable.

'Stuart,' he whispered, grabbing my arm, but not taking his eyes off her. 'You know what? She really understands me! She can read me like a book.'

'Buchanan!'

'No, listen, Stuart. You know what she said to me the first time she came up to me?'

I looked at him in anticipation. His eyes glowed. 'She said to me, "Buchanan, you look like you're in second gear …"'

11

Living in Dalkey was paradise for us all. It is a beautiful village with lovely old shops and restaurants, an ancient castle and a fine example of the Church of Ireland at its most powerful and best, St Patrick's.

I loved attending service there, especially the times when I got to play the organ. Throughout my run-around childhood I had stuck with my music lessons at whatever school I attended and eventually proved to be a reasonable singer and a competent, although not necessarily exceptional, piano player. When I was about thirteen, the vicar of a church near the army camp at Fort George in Scotland where Dad served for a while, took a liking to me and allowed me to develop my skills on the organ and it was something that I maintained from there.

Of course, having just joined the St Patrick's congregation when we moved into Dalkey, I could not expect to immediately take over the senior organ player's role. That was held firmly by a Mrs Tunbridge, more or less a position for life. She had sat on that seat pumping out *How Great Thou Art* and other much-loved fare for fifty-one years and was not going to surrender it lightly.

But I gradually worked my way into the post of assistant, filling in on the rare occasions when illness or family issues prevented her from playing, an opportunity that stood me in good stead when I successfully stood for election to the congregational committee.

I was proud of us as a growing family when we went to church every Sunday. It was a big decision for Jennifer to attend a Protestant church, but she was prepared to put aside the powerful influences of her Catholic heritage and her Buddhist beliefs for one hour a week and I really appreciated that. If I was playing the organ, it was wonderful to be able to look around and see my children all neatly dressed, sitting in a row obediently next to their beautiful mother. Such was my input, I was eventually elected to the parish committee, opening up a whole new world for me in terms of contacts and lending my support in shaping the future of the church and its community.

The hallmark of Dalkey is that it is on the seaside, with hills and cliff faces overlooking the water, the DART railway line jammed on its edge and winding roads leading south to Wexford. While Jennifer and I were walking along the shore one day, I had one of those epiphany moments that altered my life. There was a strong, flukey breeze blowing offshore and a sizable yacht was tacking its way out to sea with three people on board. Suddenly the boat started to yaw violently and looked like it was going to tip. Then the spinnaker at the front broke free and began flapping crazily in the breeze, making the boat lurch from side to side at a dangerous angle. I thought it was going to turn over. The boat was out of control and the man at the helm was in a state of panic desperately flinging the wheel one way then the other.

Then something pretty special happened. A fourth man suddenly appeared from below decks. He pushed the other man away from the wheel and grabbed it and began barking instructions. The man now freed up from his helm duties rushed forward to the bow of the boat to grab the flapping sail. Under instructions, the other two began to drop the spinnaker and trim the main-sail. Rather than flinging the wheel, the captain subtly turned it this way and that and within less than half a minute the boat was back on an even keel sailing beautifully once more. It was a marvellous performance by the skipper and I decided at that moment that I should apply the same principles to my family so that it could ride out any rough weather and quickly resolve any issues thrown at it.

The episode in Dubrovnik where I had drawn back from the dangerous abyss of adultery with Federica had confirmed my faith in myself, my belief in our marriage, and my determination to work even harder on it. Seeing this sailing episode now clarified everything further for me. I decided then and there we should look at things this way: we were all in one boat and therefore there should be only one captain. A person keeping things on an even keel no matter what challenges were thrown up. A sole tactician ensuring that the course we charted was clear to everyone. A supreme ship's master making sure we were all working smoothly as a crew and doing our appointed jobs to reach our destination. And that person should be me.

As far as I was concerned, I was logically that man. After all, that is how I had run my life up until that point and the technique had been successful, so why change now? On the other hand, Jennifer's life had been variable, episodic, bordering on the chaotic at times. From what I could see, her successes had been more the result of good luck than good management.

So, being a financial man as well, I felt it was essential that I kept an eye on every cent that went in and out of the house. Knowing from experience with clients how easy it was to slide into a financial catastrophe, I did not want to risk money being spent frivolously and unnecessarily. I worked out that the simplest way was to give Jennifer an exact amount for housekeeping each week and get her to show me the receipts after she had shopped each Friday so I could see where it had all gone. By keeping the paperwork, she could then justify any request for an increase in her allowance as prices went up, although I always tried to keep any improvement as close to the accepted inflation rate as possible.

Quite frankly I did not believe I could trust Jennifer with money. I valued every cent. But in her typical Catholic style, if she ever had any money left over she let it quickly slip through her hands. It took me a long time to realise that some of it was being handed straight on to her brother Kevin to help him finance his gambling habit at the race tracks. I was furious when I discovered this, especially as he had taken it upon himself to be her protector, thus putting him in constant friction with me. He still seemed to think that it was his job to look after her, even though Jennifer and I had long been married. I demanded that she stop wasting money on this 'loser' as I once described him. 'Have you ever heard of a successful gambler?' I asked. 'No,' I continued, answering for her. 'These fellows, they shake every one down, often embezzling money from their own firms, yet they still can't get in front! It astounds me that they spend thousands and thousands down at the betting shop, and they can never tip a winner. Then they keep trying to recover those losses and only lose more. Are they stupid, or what?'

I knew I was on rocky ground criticising Kevin because not only was he closest to Jennifer in age but he had also married her best friend Amy and so the bond was doubly strong. I think he and Amy had been forced into getting married not long after they had left school because she got pregnant. That was pretty typical of a big sprawling Catholic family; they can never control their passion and they eventually pay the price. So discussing Kevin was an area I felt I generally should leave alone unless it directly affected me. And in this case, it did.

Another thing that irked me was that a lot of the money I allotted Jennifer went on frivolous things like clothes. And what really made me angry was the number of times she would go out and buy a dress for herself and which, from what I observed, she would wear just once. Or a pair of shoes that rarely saw the light of day from amongst the dozens of others in the bottom of the closet. I don't think that this situation was helped by the fact that she was the only girl in her family and that her father had indulged her as his little princess. She grew up having what she wanted when she wanted. I decided it was my job to bring her back to reality.

She would also spend a lot of money buying school uniforms and other outfits for the children. I used to say to her, 'How many uniforms do these kids need to go to school?' As well as the financial waste of buying new clothes all the time, there was also the issue of good taste. I was happy for Jennifer to look good, as she did on the first day we met, but I felt that as we were now man and wife and also parents it was important that she presented herself appropriately. As a successful businessman, I had an image to uphold. Shortly after we had been married, I had taken her into the bedroom one day and had insisted that she throw out a lot of her clothes, particularly the ones that I felt were now demeaning for a married women to be wearing, such as the short skirts and the low-cut tops. I had laid them out on the bed to illustrate my point. 'When we go out to dinner with associates, I want you to be sociable, but not flirty,' I said.

I emphasised to her the importance of wearing sensible dresses, not provocative ones, and cutting back on the make-up so that she would not look cheap and draw the attention of other men. 'You looked beautiful the night we got married,' I would say. 'You hardly had any make-up on then.' This became something of a point of contention over the years. One night, when we were at a restaurant with Derek and a new client plus their wives, Jennifer excused herself from the table and returned from the ladies' room a few minutes later freshened up, her face caked with make-up and her lips a blaze of colour. It was that Poppy King cherry lipstick again. I was certain I had thrown every stick of it out of the house. This little rebellion only proved my point. The client sitting opposite her, who had up until then taken little notice of Jennifer, suddenly began to talk animatedly with her and she responded in kind. Before you knew it, her bubbly laugh had started to echo through the restaurant, drawing the attention of other diners. I was absolutely livid. This forced me to excuse us early and head home on the pretence that the baby-sitter, a friend of a friend who had filled in at the last minute, needed to finish up at ten o'clock because she had school exams the next day. Driving home, it took all my powers of persuasion to convince Jennifer that doing something like that only made her look stupid and cheap and reflected badly on us as a couple.

'This does not help my business, do you understand?' I said. She folded her arms, angrily pushed herself back into the seat, and stared out the window. 'I was only trying to look good for you,' she said sourly. 'Besides, you must admit that it sparked up the conversation. That dead trout opposite me had said nothing up until then. Next time I'll flash my tits at him.'

I slammed on the brakes, pulled the car over to the side of the road, leaned across and put one hand around her throat. 'What a disgusting thing to say,' I said. 'You're not only trying to look like a slut, now you're sounding like one.'

'Stuart, I …'

'Don't Stuart me!' I yelled, holding her throat firmly with one hand, while I wiped the lipstick off with the back of the other. 'See? All gone! No more cheap lipstick. Not now. Not ever!'

I let her go, got the car going again, and there was no further discussion as she sat hard up against the passenger door quietly weeping. After I had dropped her off and then driven the baby-sitter to her home nearby I returned to find that Jennifer had turned the bedroom light off and so I went downstairs and did some paperwork.

In the morning it was all I could do to get her to put the previous night's incident behind her and concentrate on our usual breakfast discussion of the upcoming day's activities, which we used to do in detail before I left for work. I appreciated her free spirit but as the ship's captain I did not want our boat to drift off course and crash on the rocks of marital misery through misinformation, indecision or lack of a clear plan. Or, worse still, rebellion. The insurance man in me insisted on taking action to prevent disasters before they occurred rather than having to clean up after they had happened. I knew all about the principle of the event after the fact. It's in the insurer's handbook.

That is why I used to phone her throughout the day. To make sure what we talked about actually happened and that she did not get distracted and do silly things or spend too much time with her friends. There was a joke in the family that you could tell the time of the day by my calls to the home landline or Jennifer's mobile.

There were four calls each day. I would ring as soon as I got to work, usually around ten past nine, just to let Jennifer know that I had arrived safely after the drive-and-park in the city and to see if the kids had got off all right to school. The mid-morning call, usually when I had a cup of coffee at 11.30 am, gave us a good opportunity to see how the day was panning out. I would then call at 2 pm. I always felt this was a good time. Lunch should be well and truly over by then and Jennifer should have had plans for dinner well in hand. As well, I was always keen to know what Jennifer had achieved so far in terms of what we had discussed that morning and what else she had to do that afternoon. The final call at 4.55 pm was opportune because it usually confirmed that the kids were now well home from school and doing their homework and I could inform Jennifer that I was either on the way home for dinner, or staying back to do some work, or heading out to see a client.

I loved to hear the sound of her voice on the end of the line. When the children were really young it was great to get first-hand news on any milestones they might have achieved, whether that was saying a first word or taking a few tentative steps. I believed my role as captain of the ship became even more important as each child came along and the relationship between Jennifer and I changed. Of course I understood that the structure of a partnership must surely alter once the first flush of unbridled romance had passed. It modifies itself to the circumstances, each individual's strengths and weaknesses becoming apparent as challenges arise and trade-offs are established to keep things moving. What was once a partner's endearing peccadillo can easily, over a period of time, transform into a very annoying habit. I accepted all that and knew that I had to respond to those situations with a mixture of wisdom, diplomacy and the ability to take change on board. I couldn't afford to let things get out of control.

Jennifer's family might have tested my patience, but they provided me with a whole new world of business contacts and potential clients. Having spent more of my childhood out of the Ireland than in, I ended up speaking with something of an English accent, which didn't necessarily endear me to the more traditional Catholic community. I had to work harder than most to get business in that sector but having links with Jennifer's family, the doors started to open. Seamus and his sons might have enjoyed making life difficult for me on a social basis, but I was family, and in a business sense they proved invaluable.

I worked hard to create more personal wealth through commercial success to make things as comfortable and as best as I could for my family. And what a time to do it. Other countries might have benefited from gold rushes or mining booms but Ireland had puttered along the poverty line until this economic rocket – the one the shark's teeth real estate agent had predicted that night at dinner – went off with a bang. Cash started flowing as employers and unions worked together, government investment boomed and women began to enter the workforce. After years of Ireland sending its people off to America, something finally began to drift back across the Atlantic – dollars. To me, the

Celtic Tiger was an odd name, taken from the Asian Tigers, such as Malaysia, Thailand and Singapore, who had their own economic miracles. Little old Ireland had never really had a 'tiger' feel about it. It had been a bit cranky at times. And physical, as seen on the sports field. And explosive, especially when old wounds re-surfaced. And dogged, particularly amongst the male population, to stick to a decision no matter how right or wrong it was.

But the Celtic Tiger it was, and how we benefited! Fitting in with my favourite credo – for every action there is an equal and opposite reaction – for every project there was an equal and appropriate underwriting. Our computer equipment had to be continually upgraded as the insurance contracts and paperwork flooded the system. Fortunately we never got into the really massive stuff such as insuring the construction of the new motorways that radiated out from the city and the giant buildings that dotted its skyline. But for a medium-size insurance agency, we flirted on the edges of the big time and some of the trailing commissions we picked up for not only insuring projects but also finding finance for clients were pretty impressive.

Our prize jewel was a project my friend Buchanan brought to our board one day, a sizeable development in Tallaght in south-west Dublin. It consisted of a four-star hotel, surrounded by luxury apartments, an entertainment complex, a lifestyle centre including swimming pool and gym, plus quality retail space. The figures looked excellent and the potential clients were blue chip, so we got involved both as insurers and, for the first time, as investors. We also encouraged some of our premium clients to put their money in. The city was awash with cash and even allowing for my inbuilt prudence on these matters, we lived very well indeed and the future could not have been rosier.

'Enjoy it,' I would say to Jennifer, when I would call her at precisely 9.10, 11.30, two o'clock and just before five. Every day.

LOVER, HUSBAND, FATHER, MONSTER

12

A nything I ever proposed, even if it seemed a bit tough, was always for the good of the family. So when Jennifer first spat the words 'control freak' at me I was absolutely shocked. I was reduced to silence for a moment and even after I had regained my composure all I could say was, 'What do you mean?'

'You look it up,' she yelled as she rushed across the landing at the top of the stairs before disappearing into the bedroom and slamming the door.

It was the climax to a rather unfortunate discussion. Robust interchanges were fairly rare around our house and I was taken by surprise. We had been invited to a party that night but the babysitter had pulled out at the very last minute. The phone call with the bad news came through just as both of us were coming down the stairs dressed for the party and awaiting her arrival. So I had decided that we would not be able to attend. But Jennifer insisted, pleaded, begged that she go, seeing as it was at the home of Pauline, one of our neighbours. 'It's just down the street, it's her fortieth birthday and it's a surprise,' she said. 'I'd just like to be there, even only at the start, just to see the look on her face. Oh, please, Stu.'

I said I didn't see how it was possible now that the babysitter had let us down at the eleventh hour, but typically Jennifer came up with a solution. 'What if I go down there now and see the first bit, the surprise part, and then I'll come back and then you can go down and we can take it in turns of looking after the children from there?'

I didn't like the idea of her walking up and down the road in the middle of the night and of us swapping roles and going in and out of houses. We would enjoy neither one nor the other. 'No,' I said, 'no.'

'Please, Stu,' she said, 'please. Rod has done so much to prepare this surprise for Pauline. He's worked so hard to keep it a secret. Besides, he's in your parish. And he *is* one of your clients.'

I thought about this for a while and finally concluded that maybe someone from the family being there wouldn't be such a bad thing after all. But to be truthful, I never really liked parties at the best of times. All that inane chit-chat about the weather, schools and property prices. Besides, I had noticed that there was a documentary on the Le Mans 24-hour race on BBC-2 and this would save me having to record it and try and find the time to watch it later. I agreed but told her not to worry about swapping over during the evening. 'I will stay home with the children for the night,' I said. I figured a quiet glass of red and watching the telly would be far more enjoyable than observing a bunch of childish forty-somethings getting screaming drunk.

'However,' I added, 'don't be late. Ten thirty at the latest.'

'Ten thirty?! But that's hardly any time at all,' she said, giving me her poor-little-me look with the girly green eyes.

'You heard. Ten thirty, that's enough time to party.'

As it turned out, staying home was a good decision on my part. I found a nice Chilean merlot at the bottom of the wine rack and the Le Mans doco was excellent. I didn't realise that Porsche had won it so many times.

But 10.30 pm came. No Jennifer. Then 10.35 and then 10.40. By 10.50, I was concerned. Not so much about her safety rather that Jennifer had made a promise and now she had broken it. This was typical. That insidious Wendy, her best friend, was probably down there at Pauline and Rod's, whispering in one ear about what she should do with her life while that pesky Karena, her so-called guru, would be telling her something else in the other. And who knows who else was slathering attention on her. I knew Rod's brother Alan would have been there – a dangerous individual at the best of times. He had a ramshackle marriage and was a notorious womaniser, just the type that would start chatting up someone as pretty and vivacious as my wife and coaxing her towards a bedroom. I disliked it intensely when other men started casting their eyes towards her. I knew what they were after. Fortunately I had insisted she dress demurely before she left. Although, you never knew, the minute she got out the door she probably slapped some of that red lipstick on and hitched her skirt up to show her legs. That's the sort of thing she would do. You could never trust her.

So, the appointed return time had come and gone, and no appearance. What to do? I decided I would give her half an hour's grace. But by 11.05 I had had enough of peering through the front window to see if she was coming home. After checking to see that all three kids were sound asleep, I marched briskly the eighty metres down the road to Rod's place. On the way I began figuring out a way to get Jennifer out of there quickly and without much fuss. I stood on the door-step and thought about it for a while before finally ringing the bell. I knew what I had to say.

Naturally enough, there was a great cheer from everyone when I entered. All the men kept slapping me on the back and offering me a pint or a whiskey. But the women, of course, knew immediately that my sudden appearance was not right. I was in charge of the children, so how come I had now turned up at the party without them? Had I somehow magically organised the impossible at that hour of the night – someone else to take over? Or had I done the unthinkable and left them on their own in the house? As I correctly assumed, when Jennifer made her way through the crowd, I knew that that thought would be foremost in her mind.

'What's the matter?' she said anxiously. 'The kids! Why aren't you with them?'

'It's Molly,' I said. Her face at once fell concerned.

'It's all right,' I quickly added. 'But she won't settle. She started crying just after you left and hasn't stopped since.' I looked downcast.

'Oh, you poor thing, Stu,' said Pauline, stepping forward and touching me lightly on the arm. 'Having to put up with that all night while we're down here having fun.' She looked around at the other guests. 'Isn't he wonderful, everyone?' I had found an ally amongst the enemy.

'Yes, yes,' came a smattering of voices.

'I didn't know what to do,' I added forlornly.

'Awww,' said my newfound audience.

'So I thought I'd best take the risk for just a few seconds and come down and get you, darling. She keeps saying she wants her mummy. You know how it is, Mam is number one.'

There were murmurs of both concern and approval, although out of the corner of my eye I detected that damn Wendy shaking her head. Someone produced Jennifer's coat and after a series of quick goodbyes – 'Let us know if everything's all right, Stu,' said Pauline – we headed quickly and silently out into the darkness and down the narrow footpath to our home. I opened the door and Jennifer raced in, cocking her ear for the sound of Molly as she headed for the stairs with me right behind her. 'I can't hear anything,' she said, stopping for an instant.

'No,' I said, grabbing her by the shoulder and turning her around to face me. 'She's been perfect all night.'

'What ... what do you mean?'

I leaned forward, right into her face. I felt it was important that she understood how strongly I felt about this.

'When I say ten thirty, I mean ten thirty, okay?' I said. 'Not a minute more.'

'What? Is that what this is about?'

'Of course it is! I said ten thirty, didn't I? And now it is well after eleven. That is not good enough.'

'You made up that story to get me back here? You bastard!'

That was enough. I have never been so angry in all my life. No one speaks to me like that. I felt myself moving my hand from her shoulder around to her throat.

'Are you calling me a liar, now?' I said.

'No, no.'

'You just did.'

'No, I didn't, honestly, Stu.'

'Didn't you just say that I had made up a story?'

'Yes, but I didn't mean …'

I tightened my hand around her throat.

'You didn't mean what? To say that I was a liar? I think you just did,' I said, pushing her hard up against the wall. I felt it was important that she clearly understood that I was not happy with all this. First, she was late, now she was saying I told lies.

'Stuart, please, I was concerned about Molly. You said …'

'Hah! Molly! Your little princess. I knew that would get you out of there quickly, away from all those men hanging around leering at you. Would you have been so anxious if it had've been one of the boys? I don't think so.'

I banged her head against the wall. She winced as the back of it hit the solid plaster with a thump.

'Huh?' I demanded.

'Yes, yes, of course I would,' she said lamely. 'They're all important to me.'

'Now who's the liar?' I said. 'It's always you and Molly. Molly and you. That's all you care about. Apart from the little game Molly and I have together, that's it as far as I'm concerned. The pair of you have set up your own separate unit within the family.'

I felt that I had made my point so I let her go and she gasped for breath. 'Go to bed,' I said.

'Stu, please.'

'Go to fucking bed!!' I shouted. She put her head down, turned and walked slowly up the stairs.

'And don't dare do anything like this again,' I added, as she reached the landing.

It was then she turned and hissed, 'Control freak!'

I could not utter a word for a moment, I was so shocked that she would be so brazen. And even then, after I had regained my composure, all I could say was, 'What do you mean by that?' as she headed across the landing at the top of the stairs.

'You look it up,' she yelled, before disappearing into the bedroom, slamming the door. I heard the key turn in the lock. I was boiling angry and actually started up the stairs but I knew that it would be pointless going up there battering on the door and waking the kids. So I went into the front lounge, poured a whiskey, pulled out the divan bed and settled in for the night. It was a place I was getting accustomed to. Besides, I had a bit of research to do and it wasn't long before I found what I needed. Amongst the shelves groaning with Jennifer's books on New Age philosophy, Eastern mysticism and God knows what else, I spotted a book on psychology that presumably one of her 'advisors' had given her. I scanned through the index and looked up 'control.'

'See "Emotional Abuse",' it said. I flipped through, found the page, sat down and began to read.

'Examples of emotional abuse,' it read, 'include when one person in a partnership, more often than not the male, unilaterally decides when and where the other person can go, who she can see and what sort of friends she can have. With the main aim of socially isolating her, he will disallow her from developing a support system by regulating who she can call on the phone or write to on email, as well as determining whether she can go out and get a job or not. This latter often includes selecting what type of employment. He will often scrutinise and make decisions on guests she invites into their home.'

Well, I thought, you couldn't blame me for that last bit, about who should be allowed into *my* home. Some of those women, particularly Jennifer's Buddhist gurus, were getting too influential for comfort as far as I was concerned and knew far too much about our lives. They acted like our place was theirs. I might have made it clear that I did not like them around. But did I stop them? Of course I didn't.

As for Jennifer getting a job, well we had both unilaterally agreed it was best that she be the manager of the home. And as for that other stuff about disallowing support systems and so on, well, as they said in the book, they were only 'examples'. Every home is different. When you are the captain, it is your duty to keep tabs on the crew so they don't get into trouble, lose focus or become rebellious. A good vessel only sails successfully if everyone clearly understands the captain's approach and does not deviate from that. You can't have it both ways. I used to try and explain to Jennifer that that was why we had such a wonderful family unit, lived in a lovely home in a beautiful suburb, had a sound financial set-up with excellent prospects and engendered the appreciation and envy of those all around us. 'You can't successfully establish that scenario when there is mutiny on board or people deliberately flouting the commander's orders,' I would say. 'That is why great skippers, like Admiral Nelson, achieved so much.'

I admired Nelson. He was one of my heroes. He was an inspiration to his men, dedicated to the cause and a leader who planned his tactics carefully. A very strong man that not even injury could stop through many campaigns. Even in death he was the victor.

I read on. There was more balderdash about emotional abuse and promoting lack of self-esteem. Something about 'death by a thousands cuts' and how things build up gradually over the years. 'Often, when the alienated person seeks help, she gives examples of what has happened. These, when isolated and mentioned by themselves, don't necessarily sound threatening. But when they occur continually over the years, and taken as a whole, they combine to create a fearful environment.'

There you go, I thought, that's exactly what I mean. These are all little incidents. Easily gotten over. Soon erased from the memory. Each individual situation should be taken on its merits. Something goes wrong, an inquiry is held, discipline is meted out, life goes on. End of story. Get on with it.

Just as I suspected, everything was quiet in the morning. Shipshape, in fact.

13

Women actually talk to each other. Men don't. When women get together, they plumb the most personal of issues right down to the very depths. When men get together, we skim across the surface. We skirt around the issue, we talk about inanities, we only get to the point when we really, really have to. At a party, women will talk about the latest additions to their families, the progression of their children, the hot news on personal relationships, the impact commercial and government price rises are having on the household budget and what great bargains are going around. Men will discuss the English Premier League.

Under all our macho bravado and camaraderie, there is a lot of confusion, fear, loathing, mistrust and puzzlement between men. Women understand women; but men really do not understand men.

That is how I have found things in life, particularly in the club atmosphere. Clubs are good in that they provide an opportunity to network. You can set up business contacts, meet people in allied industries and cultivate someone who might prove invaluable down the track. So it is worth persisting with. But it is all so artificial.

One problem is the pecking order. Clubs tend to attract ego-tripping A-types who want to be the boss and push other people around. They see the club as theirs. So they take it over, re-fashion it in their own image and then insist that everyone fits into the environment that they have so graciously created. A new member has to go along with that agenda and play the game or otherwise he will quickly find out he is going to have a very quiet and quite possibly miserable time.

Jennifer's family introduced me to the golf scene and at first it seemed like a great idea. A nice game out on a beautifully manicured course. A few drinks with everyone afterwards. And above all, the opportunity to make contacts and connections to help grow the business. But it was not enjoyable; it was hard work. Even I, as a conservative man and a stickler for rules, found it stultifying, almost scary. Not only out on the course, where the draconian rules of the game made the insurer's handbook look like child's play, but in the clubhouse where the pecking order was at its worst. I concentrated so hard on fitting in and not making a mistake that I never really relaxed and enjoyed it. I used to look at some of the older members slapping each other on the back and laughing at some lame joke and think, 'Will I ever get to the stage? Will I ever really enjoy myself here? Will I ever be accepted?' To succeed, it's as if you have to strip off the 'real you' at the front door and put on the cloak of the 'club you' before you walk inside.

When I played, my hands used to be sweaty throughout the round, particularly if it was some sort of four-ball competition and I had a partner relying on me. I bought the best clubs, listened attentively during my lessons and practised as much as I could. On the practice range I could hit it straight as a die. But on the course, under the watchful eyes of others, I could rarely relax. I duffed shots, I hooked drives, I missed the simplest of putts. And when you do it once you get so down on yourself that it makes you more flustered and you commit more mistakes. Ones of the worst kind. Etiquette mistakes. 'Not your honour, old man,' they would say as I inadvertently teed up first. 'You grounded your club on the sand in the bunker, that's a two-shot penalty,' just as I was about to strike. 'Don't you remember, Stuart? The rule at this hole is, we mark our ball, step to the side of the green, call the next group on to play their tee shot and then we putt out. Right?'

In the clubhouse, certain people sat automatically at invisibly designated tables, rules of dress were severely followed, staff were treated with courteous disdain. For newcomers, the principal role seemed to be to pay homage to the older members. With my inability to quickly connect to people on a social basis, it was a long and painful process. One day, after realising that I had played the game for two and a half years and my handicap had barely improved and the Captain still did not know my name, I wrote out my resignation. But that evening with the letter still in my jacket pocket as I ordered a drink at the bar, a member who had never spoken to me before quietly sidled up and said, 'You're in insurance, aren't you? I've got some business I'd like to put your way.' He turned out to be one of my best clients and so I tore the quit letter up and never sent it.

Things improved. Connections lead to connections. Through one of the golf members I was lured into the service club scene. My experiences in the Lions ran somewhat parallel with what was happening on the golf course. I made a lot of money out of signing many a good Lion up for a policy but I was always on the fringe of the real club circle. I attended every meeting, drank cheap wine with the best of them and put on an apron and cooked at the Saturday morning sausage sizzle outside the local hardware store. I was an enthusiastic participant of every fund-raiser team and major project sub-committee. At one stage I was even the tail-twister, the theatrical player in a sequence where members at the dinner meeting are dobbed in for tardiness, stupidity or poor performance. They are fined and have to throw a few coins into a money box. I tried to do this with the best of intentions and with as much humour and élan as I could muster. And I stuck with it for months, even after one night, when I went to the gents' toilet and was sitting in a cubicle and two others came in for a leak and one said to the other, 'That Stuart fellow. Did you see him tonight? He's a nice enough lad, but a bit of a try-hard.'

There are a lot of others who come up against this brick wall and who give it away. Me being me, inheriting some of father's military doggedness and having survived tough times at boarding college, I hung in there because I thought it was worth it business-wise, and therefore in the long term good for me, Jennifer and the family.

But in moments of self-realisation I knew that, even though I could hold up a reasonably good conversation on most topics, I did not have the required mental nimbleness and wherewithal to fully cope with these people, even when they were being overbearing and quite bullying in their superficial, polite, clubby way. It dawned on me that I was surrounded by people, but I had no real friends; that I gave off the impression that I was a member of the A-team, but I was not even on the reserves bench; that I might be strong in my convictions, but I didn't have that upfront, blaggard persona to captivate a whole audience. I was more a one-on-one man. And apart from work, and perhaps on the church committee where most of the members were so old they hardly knew what was going on, the only place that I could confidently express my views and get what I wanted was at home. That was where I was the boss. Where I could exercise my authority. Where I could be in control. Home. That was my club.

Now, in my club, on my home turf, I will declare that I could be a bit insistent sometimes, occasionally demanding and sometimes over the top in my search for perfection. There were times that I regret that my anger spilled over. It was just that I wanted things to be 'right.' I would never mean to physically hurt Jennifer. That was the last thing on my mind. But there were moments, flash-points, when she would take me right to the edge. I had been originally attracted to her for, amongst many things, her beauty. But after we were married I didn't think that I should have to publicly share that beauty with others.

That is why I would get very cross with her when she wore dresses that were too short or tops that were low-cut, or when she applied heavy make-up or plastered on that bright red lipstick. Or when I detected her sending out the wrong signals to other men. I knew when she was doing it. I could tell. I felt she was doing herself and therefore me and the family a disservice, an injustice. She was better than that. I felt it was my duty to make it clear to her that she was only demeaning herself, and therefore me, by doing it. In outlining my view, perhaps I should not have physically intimidated her. I tried not to. But sometimes, when she was obviously not listening to what I was trying to explain, or showing signs of being resentful, or downright denying what was the obvious truth, I would suddenly find myself restraining her before I knew what I was doing. It was all so quick. The judo experience had sharpened my reflexes and trained me to take rapid action.

But sometimes she would deliberately push things too far and I would respond accordingly. It was just a natural response to strike her. Not premeditated. But I had to make my view on the situation clear. She knew the rules. It was up to her to conduct herself accordingly.

Anyone who has been down this path will tell you that pressures build up in marriages. External influences, elements that you don't even remotely consider in the first flush of warm romance, start to come into play and cause havoc. As each child comes along, the mother, the one bearing the brunt of the ever-growing domestic scene, gets more tired. Things like intimacy and love-making take a back seat. That was okay, I could understand that. I may have had a decent sperm count, I may have wanted sex more times than we actually did have, but don't forget I had endured a lot of years without a long-term partner. Or for that matter, any sort of girlfriend. So I was used to lengthy celibate periods. Nevertheless having now been married for some years, it could get very frustrating at times when the weeks went by and we never had sex. That was when the verbal spats would flare and I would, being so frustrated, take action. I would insist we make love for both my sanity and for Jennifer's too. Feeling the rigidity of her body I knew she was just going through the routine and waiting for it to finish. That only made me push harder in the hope that her resistance would somehow melt away and the joyous, cohesive love we used to make would magically return. Sometimes I used to think, 'If only she drank. A couple of glasses of wine, instead of that fucking fruit juice, and she might relax and be happy and enjoy it instead of being so damn uptight.'

I began to think, 'Could it be? That I have done the business, sired the children that she so desperately wanted and now she has cast me aside? That my services are not needed any more? That what is being left unsaid is, "Thank you Stuart, you've done a good job and you may now bugger off?"'

Then the other side of the argument would pop into my head. 'Surely that is not what has happened. That she targeted me solely for this role? She couldn't be that cynical, could she?' After a while, as things limped along, the thought began to eat into me that I was the innocent patsy in Jennifer's grand plan. A scheme of deception to achieve conception. Picking any bloke off the street to be the stud because all previous attempts had failed for varying reasons and she was fast running out of time. And I happened to be the one! Ultimately I began to think, 'Well, if that's what you've done and that's the way you want it, my dearest, then here it is.' And so our rare lovemaking became a dry, emotionless experience, a battle of wills, not much more than combat under the duvet. Usually very quick, often painful for both of us as I thrust in and out, hard and strong and angry, simmering with frustration, having to wear an infernal condom because she wouldn't take the pill. Goddam it, she could be so diffident, so difficult, so determined, when she wanted to be. Often she would lay there with her head turned to one side, looking away from me, like an uninvolved prostitute waiting for the commercial transaction to conclude so she could collect her fee and depart. That's when I would turn her over and enter her from behind, which gave me some feeling of control, even though I knew that beneath me, on all fours, she would be staring into the gloom at the bed-head, waiting for it to end. Sometimes I did not know whether the moan she gave out each time I pushed was one of pleasure or pain. They always say there is a fine line between those two disparate sensations, but quite frankly I did not give a damn which one it was. I just wanted relief.

In post-coital coldness, as we lay next to each other staring silently at the ceiling, I used to think I would have been better off on my own with a copy of a men's magazine and a firm grip with my right hand, just like I had done when I successfully produced the sperm sample that proved our troubled baby-making experiences were not my fault. So, after a while, I started doing just that. 'Damn it,' I thought, 'she reduced me to doing that for her, when it was unecessary! So why not just do it for me? Everyone else around here seems to be looking after number one, so why shouldn't I?'

I had heard about the proliferation of pornography on the internet, even overhearing Buchanan telling one of his friends one day about how 'they do feckin' everythin' on those sites, those women, they take it every feckin' which way'. But being so useless with the computer and not having one in my study at home anyway, I opted for the more traditional method. I began to quietly cruise my way through less than salubrious newsagents, ones that I would not normally frequent, discreetly buying magazines of that ilk and using them as a source of inspiration to relieve my frustration. To the casual observer, I suppose it would not be the most edifying image, that of the respected family man, successful business executive, pillar of the church and regular contributor of thoughtful correspondence to the letters pages of our better newspapers, hiding in his locked study, hunched over a picture of a naked spread-eagled woman, breathing heavily as he tugs rhythmically on his hardened penis, imagining that he is having sex with her, until he can no longer control himself and comes, spraying all over her picture, before collapsing back in the chair, replete with overwhelming physical satisfaction but racked with gnawing shame and embarrassment.

I had mixed feelings about it. Sometimes I felt awkward, sometimes I simply felt that it was the appropriate thing to do considering the circumstances, while at other times an exhilarating feeling of immense power would come over me and I would truly imagine myself having domineering sex with this dirty little slut spread out before me in full-colour gloss. 'I'm going to fuck you, you bitch,' I would moan quietly as I became more erect, even recalling the old play on words based on my surname that had dogged me in my younger days. 'Take this, you whore,' I would hiss. 'From one Hoare to another! Ha! How do you like that?'

I would have continued buying the magazines, but one day, as I was hovering around the mens' magazine section of a SPAR far away from home base, out of the corner of my eye I saw a parishioner I vaguely knew observing me. I quietly moved away from the racks, trying to give off the air that I had stumbled down the aisle by accident, and bought some bread and milk and exited casually, pretending not to see him. I think that I saved face, but it spooked me. What an embarrassment if that story had got around church circles.

One of my more successful techniques was to imagine that I did take up the offer made by the gorgeous Federica that night in the hotel in Dubrovnik, something that, as the gulf inexorably grew between Jennifer and me, I began to regret not doing. The image would quickly come to mind of my Swiss love goddess lying naked on the bed beckoning me, her pure white skin glistening in the subdued light of the hotel room. Instead of fleeing, I could see myself confidently taking those last few steps across the floor to strip off and join her. As I would tug harder and get more excited and my mind would begin to race, I could almost smell her, feel her, touch every part of her fit, athletic body as we drove each other on to a crashing imaginary climax. 'Oh, Federica,' I would whisper in the darkened study. 'What a woman. What a lover. What an idiot I was to walk away from you.' I suppose the good thing was that after I came, the pressure valve was released and it calmed me down for days.

Other things also built up the tension, Jennifer's fascination with all things vegetarian proving to be particularly frustrating. I was brought up a meat-and-vegetables man and I will die one. That is the way my Mum cooked, that is what my Dad loved, and that is what I adored. To me, a nice piece of medium-rare fillet steak or some beautifully done pork chops or even grilled sausages along with potatoes in one form or other and some sort of vegetable, preferably peas, provided a good, sound, enjoyable diet. I have got nothing against lentils and hummus and fake curries made out of Brussel sprouts and all that other Asian malarkey, but it gets you down night after night. One of the best release valves was when we would go down to one of the local restaurants at Dalkey and I could have a steak and a decent bottle of red. Things like that plus a nightly glass or two of a good single-malt whiskey by myself in my study, along with a vintage copy of *Hustler* or an imaginative creation of a wild night with Federica kept me going, made me think it was all worthwhile, helped me keep my sanity, stopped me from getting too serious and too over-bearing. And that was important to me.

14

I absolutely, totally, firmly believe the entire blame for whatever friction or difficulty that erupted in our house should be laid directly at the feet of Wendy Cunningham.

Wendy was Jennifer's best friend. I was convinced she only developed the relationship to see what she could get out of it. Mainly my money. But Jennifer thought she was a wonderful person. They had met via the Buddhist movement and Wendy, who had built up a career as a personal development consultant and business coach, became not only Jennifer's pal but also her confidante and advisor. This annoyed me greatly.

Wendy was a New Zealander and, from what I could see, she not only came from a different country but another galaxy. She was tiny, with short-cropped dark hair, flawless olive skin and huge, saucer-shaped brown eyes that peered at you with an annoying glint that said, 'I-know-the-secret-to-the-meaning-of-life-and-you-don't.' Even though she was tiny she made up for her lack of size with her outfits, mainly voluminous caftans in layers of clashing reds, yellows, blues and greens. And the jewellery! She clanked and rattled wherever she went amid a sea of gold, silver and emeralds. Jangling bracelets on both wrists, chains around her neck, fingers covered in rings, giant hoop ear-rings you could throw a basketball through. Buchanan, long recognised in the industry for the accuracy of his valuations, reckoned she was lumping around approximately one-third of her own body weight in precious metals.

But while Wendy was the tiniest of persons, she made the biggest of impressions. She would turn up anywhere, whether in a private home or a public place, and float around like some sort of mystical goddess, her dress billowing in the breeze, her jewellery jangling and her mouth going non-stop. When I would walk in the door at home in the evening, I would immediately know if Wendy had been in the house sometime during the day. Even if she had left hours before, I could still detect the residue of that curious musk-like smell that always seemed to accompany those alternative types; that sickly-sweet aroma, like someone had lit a joss stick or smoked marijuana.

Wendy was the one who took over the production and sale of Jennifer's doleful little '*Inner Me*' books and self-help camps, after I insisted that she give up that trite little business and concentrate on the important issue of solely running the house. As a result, the pair of them shared a very close bond, one that made me edgy, suspicious and occasionally angry. I often got the impression Jennifer would tell Wendy about things that she had planned for the family even before she would tell me. Sometimes Wendy would be there when I got home and you could tell from the smirk as she was leaving that she knew Jennifer was about to broach something with me. Some scheme or idea that the pair of them had hatched, and you could bet that she would phone

Jennifer the next day to find out how I had responded to it.

Having arrived in Ireland from New Zealand in the late 1980s as a back-packer, Wendy had never left and had built up quite an operation advising clients, including business people, on how to improve their lives. As the Celtic Tiger flourished she had made a killing. Booming companies awash with cash would send their employees to see her with a view to improving their self-esteem, performance and organisational skills.

I used to laugh quietly to myself about that, because I knew that Wendy's own personal life was absolutely chaotic. She was typical of those types who got paid a fortune to tell other people how to run their lives and yet couldn't keep their own on track. She had been married twice, was estranged from her only daughter and was being sued for libel over one of her books. At one stage she had a restraining order placed on her then boyfriend, a moody, former Ukrainian soccer player she had met at a sports management conference in Kiev. Then typically she had the order taken off! I know that because she was at our home one day and her mobile phone rang and she went into another room and screamed down the line at him, threatening to hang up, although noticeably she didn't. Then, when he got in first and ended the call, she burst into tears and tried to phone him back. That fraught, meaningless relationship raged for months until it reached its logical explosion. After she bawled on Jennifer's shoulder for a week, she suddenly brightened up, as she had found the next poor sap to go fifteen rounds with, a millionaire businessman with a yacht.

Despite the significant fees she pulled, although why people would pay to go and hear her speak I do not know, plus the sales of her books and DVDs, her finances were always in a mess. She was either flush with cash or desperately needing to borrow money in order to pay her bills, shore up an overdrawn account or stabilize a melting credit card. She swung wildly from total control of her affairs to sheer incompetence. While she was supremely confident in her own abilities, she was, as far as I was concerned, quite daffy.

I saw a bit of one of her presentations on video once, an eclectic and frequently bizarre ramble through where we were, where we should be and how to get there. She talked about releasing yourself from the shackles of life and following your whimsical spirit rather than any carefully set course charted by your strict moral compass.

She spoke in elliptical loops about personal development, individual growth and seizing the opportunity. She had every feel-good catchphrase down pat. I laughed out loud at one: 'To capture the delicate butterfly of life, you need to use the gossamer net of love.' She sold her books, videos, beads, bracelets, incense sticks and other tat from a little shop in south Dublin where she also ran workshops in a room up above.

A local lout sprayed graphiti over her shop front once, reading 'Buddhism – a big barrel of bollocks.' In typical style, Wendy said that if she found out who the perpetrator was she would counsel him, try and discover the deep-seated issue that was causing him such angst and present him with viable solutions. Jennifer said if she found him she would make him clean it off and then take him to a Buddhist temple for a peaceful interlude where he could re-discover his inner-self. I said that if I ever came across him, I'd pat him on the back and give him a tenner ...

I used to say to Jennifer, 'Let me paraphrase Princess Diana. There are three people in this marriage – you, me and that bloody Kiwi friend of yours.'

There was a fourth person hovering on the edge, too – Karena, some sort of upper level member of the Buddhist movement. Somewhere along the line she had been appointed Jennifer's official guru. Apparently each member has one. As Buchanan said to me one day when they all traipsed out of the house, 'How many feckin' people do you need to tell you how to run your life?'

For someone like me who enjoyed following the simple directions supplied by our local vicar in his sermons and who took the Bible as Gospel – quote something to me out of the Good Book that you can genuinely prove is not relevant to today's society and I will give you a million euro – this was anathema.

At the end of the day Karena might have been a bit more professional than Wendy. She gave off the air of being more discreet and only taking on board the central core of the issue, out of which she would deduce a solution. But like Wendy she wheedled her way in and pretty soon knew practically everything about Jennifer, me, our relationship, our family and our hopes and dreams. I did not like that. I believed in what my father used to say in his typical military style: 'What goes on inside the barracks, stays inside the barracks.' As well, Jennifer used to pass business, personal and financial information on to Karena that I had given to her in private. This concerned me greatly. 'You don't know who she will tell!' I would say to Jennifer.

'Karena is a practicing, professional guru,' Jennifer would reply. 'She's sworn to secrecy. It's exactly the same as a doctor-patient relationship.'

'Don't make me laugh!'

'She's an acknowledged spiritual guide.'

'Ha! She's got a certificate from some witch doctor out of the Kenyan jungle, or wherever she comes from, printed off on a photocopier and stuck on her wall with Blu-Tack. I bet you she gets on the tom-toms and relays everything about us to her students and anyone else within earshot.'

Those conversations always resulted in Jennifer storming off in tears and it would take a while to placate her. Most times, it wan't even worth trying. It's just that I cannot stand self-appointed gurus. All they do is make the answers up as they go. They are gullible enough to believe that stuff in the first place then shrewd enough to recognise its opportunities and finally wily enough to set themselves up as high priests and lord it over poor devils who have not got the wherewithal to think for themselves. Jennifer virtually lay at her feet and hardly moved without her permission. 'What do you think about this, Karena? What do you think about that, Karena? What should I do here, Karena? Can I go and have a pee now, Karena?' Don't make me laugh. It was all a big con and people were stupid enough to buy into it.

In fact, I'm sure Jennifer discussed the most intimate of details of our relationship with Karena and Wendy, including our love-making - when it happened. One day when Wendy was there I dropped some papers on the floor as I came into the kitchen and uttered, 'Blimey.' Wendy burst into hysterical laughter. The look that flashed between her and Jennifer said it all.

I questioned Jennifer about it when Wendy was gone but she assured me that she had never told anyone anything about something as precious and personal as my response when I climaxed. Balderdash. I knew she had. In fact, after a while I realised that Wendy was not the only one in on that little 'joke'. I came home early and unannounced one day – I used to do that occasionally just to see if everything was running smoothly – and Jennifer and her friends from the mother's group were in the kitchen down the back chatting over coffee. Just as I quietly slipped through the front door, one of them ended her sentence with 'Blimey' and they all burst into hysterical laughter. After I had put my briefcase down and hung up my coat and scarf and appeared at the kitchen door, the laughing suddenly stopped, there were red faces everywhere, and they all decided it was time to take their kids and leave. I heard a couple of them unsuccessfully trying to stifle giggles as they went up the hallway.

Jennifer's revelation of my personal traits made me very angry. I felt any other self-respecting husband would have been quite within his rights to be furious too.

When I asked her about it later that evening, Jennifer eventually admitted that, yes, she had told 'the girls', as she called them, a few 'little things' about our lives.

'But we all do!' she said. 'We all tell each other about our husbands and their endearing foibles. There's nothing wrong with that, it's all done with love.'

Love? I stormed off to bed and it was ages before we made that again.

15

The death of the Celtic Tiger came so quickly it caught all of us on the hop. From riding an economic high one day, virtually the next day over-inflated prices were falling around our ears and the banks, including the Bank of Ireland and the Anglo Irish Bank, were revealing enormous debts. Even as a great supporter of the Government I had to admit that Fianna Fáil was tired and had been left stranded and flat-footed. I had always been a loyal follower of Bertie Ahern when he was Taoiseach, often showing my support by writing letters to the papers praising his efforts for 'conjuring up the great economic miracle that has transformed Ireland from a penniless country to a European powerhouse.'

But when the US merchant banks began to fold under the pressure of the sub-prime loan defaults and Wall Street crashed and our banks had the stuffing knocked out of them, the money dried up overnight. The cranes on the development sites suddenly stopped moving, no longer busily lifting the building materials up and down the multi-level projects that had mushroomed all over the country. This to me was the eeriest symbol of the bust. Silhouetted against the Dublin evening sky, they looked like giant mechanical giraffes stilled by some mysterious economic virus. A contractor told me it was cheaper to leave them there rather than take them down and return them to home base.

I started getting very anxious when the headlines began blaring about the stock market collapse, the banks bordering on bankruptcy and the money drying up. I became even more concerned when it was obvious that this was impacting on property development all over Dublin. My fears reached an all time high when Buchanan rang me at home one evening, exceedingly agitated.

'I've just got off the phone,' he said anxiously. 'Work has stopped at Tallaght!'

'What!' I said. 'The whole fucking lot? You told us it was bullet-proof. The hotel, the entertainment, the leisure, the accommodation, the retail space. A great mix, you told us. It couldn't go wrong, no matter what else went belly-up.'

My hand started to tremble on the phone. 'Can we get this going again?'

'No,' came the voice. 'Not for the moment anyway. I spoke to Frank. He said he's got no money and can't pay the people we already owe, much less keep pushing on with the building. He locked the gate this afternoon and sent 'em all home. That's it, Stuart. Feckin' hell. I'm sorry.'

I mumbled thanks, told him we would have to meet in the morning to see what we could do, and hung up. The tears started to well in my eyes. What had I done? I may not have been lured into some foolish exercise like buying an investment holiday flat in Bulgaria sight unseen, like many other Irishmen riding the Tiger had, but I had poured a lot of money into this project. My own personal money.

It was all too much for me. I sat down, put my head in my hands and started sobbing. Hearing this Jennifer came into the room. 'What's the matter?' she said concerned.

I looked up at her, tried to open my mouth, but found it difficult to say anything.

'What is it?' she said anxiously, coming over to me. 'Something wrong with your Da?'

'No.'

'My Da, then? He hasn't got cancer or something?'

'No.'

'Well, what is it? Have *you* got cancer?'

I looked up at her sadly, trying to pick up my strength. I felt that there could not be anything harder for a husband to tell his wife than this.

'Tallaght. The project. It's stopped. We've lost thousands.'

'Oh! Is that all?' she replied immediately, her look of anxiety converting straight into one of relief. 'I thought it was something important, someone sick or something. But it's only about money.'

She put her arm around me. 'There, there. Don't worry, you'll get it back.' And she walked off! I looked up as she left the room, my mouth wide open, and shook my head. Her naïve reaction only made me feel more depressed. 'She just doesn't get it,' I thought.

I was still dispirited the next morning, but Buchanan was positively downcast because he knew it was on his recommendation that the firm should get involved in the development, not only as insurers, but also as investors. While he had to sort out how he was going to defend his position and salvage something of his reputation, the situation presented me with a big headache on three levels. First, our company had provided the insurance on it. Now, with the developer almost certainly going bankrupt, there was going to be a lot of angst, paperwork, threats, writs and claims flying around. Fortunately we had hived a lot of it off to an insurance underwriter and the main damage to us would be a blow to our morale and a kick to our credibility. It's something you don't want to get involved in. I rang Frank, the project manager, hoping he might have some good news, but he was short, sharp and to the point. 'I'm lookin' for a new job meself right now, Stuart,' he said.

Secondly, I had encouraged some hand-picked, highly-valued clients of ours to invest in the project and would now have the difficult task of advising them that in all likelihood they would never see their cash again. Just like me. This was going to be a sensitive operation so I figured the best thing was that I should not take the brunt of it all. As he was the original proponent of the idea, I insisted Buchanan come along to the meeting so that they could crucify him.

He didn't exactly endear himself with his opening salvo, chucking aside the carefully written apologetic script that Derek and I had devised and instead going in boots and all. 'Well, no one, not even the best financial brains in the world, could have predicted this,' he roared. 'That sub-prime crap in America has done us all in. You wouldn't think they would give loans to feckin' eedjits like that, would you? Most of the fat bastards couldn't get out of their own feckin' way, much less pay a mortgage, the lard-arses.'

Derek leaned forward and whispered, 'Jayzus, Buchanan, don't hold back will ya?'

And it was on. A man stood up and said, 'Don't try and make excuses, you feckin' thieves, we want our money back,' and a tirade of complaints hit us like a tornado.

'I'd prefer hot needles poked into my eyeballs than this,' Buchanan whispered as yet another aggrieved participant stood up at the back of the conference room to give us a blast, roaring that we had 'promised the world, but lost the lot.' Many of them were small investors, first timers, couples who had put in five, maybe ten thousand euro. They were extremely shocked and disappointed that their initial move into the exciting world of high finance had brought them only pain and loss, particularly as when they signed up the Tiger was roaring and the prospects for strong returns were excellent. 'It's not worth the damn paper it's printed on,' one wife said angrily as she threw down the beautifully-bound, four-colour prospectus which featured a photo of a yuppie couple lovingly walking across the designer square past a modernist fountain towards the smiling concierge at the revolving door of their chic apartment block. Fortunately I was able to calm many of them down and regain some trust by offering reductions on their next insurance policy premiums.

Thirdly, there were the bigger investors to consider. They had split into two camps. The experienced 'old money' types who shrugged, patted me on the back and said, 'Bad luck, lad, not your fault,' and sauntered off into the evening air. They knew, as the old saying goes, never to put all your eggs in one basket. Always keep plenty in reserve to fight another day. That's why they have old money and plenty of it.

But the boots-and-all 'new money' tyros were not happy at the prospect of having to hand back the keys of the Maserati and down-sizing their luxury living conditions. They gave us a nasty pasting before they stormed out. Several threatened litigation including one who mentioned a notorious 'no-win, no-fee' Dublin barrister that he was going to hire to come after us.

'Good luck,' said Buchanan without batting an eyelid. 'He's gone to the wall, too ...'

But the worst part for me was that I had put my own money in and like everybody else, had to face up to the prospect of kissing it goodbye. When we had a chance to sit down together, I told Jennifer that it was a turn of events that no one could have predicted and that as a family we would now have to pull our collective belt in. I would have to trim back on her weekly domestic allowance, I told her.

The down-trodden, flame-haired, bog-Irish Catholic in her flared up like an aggrieved dragon. This, she considered, was very unfair. 'What's all this got to do with how we live?' she said. 'That was money I never saw anyway. It was cash you had locked up for years until you put it into this. So now it's gone, bad luck. You've still got your company and your car and your income and your commissions. And your house and your family! Why should the children and I suffer simply because of one business deal that's gone wrong?'

I tried to explain to her that it wasn't that simple.

'It's more complicated than that,' I said soothingly. 'You see, as you are not au fait with high finance ...'

'Oh, don't start that,' she interrupted. 'Don't give me that rubbish about me being the poor little housewife locked away at home who knows nothing about the big brave world of corporate business. I've got more degrees than you have, remember, and from a real university, too, not some tin-pot night school!'

'What? You be careful what you say, darling.'

'Careful? I've worked for bigger, more successful companies than your little operation, Stuart, and if I wasn't enjoying being with the kids, I'd have my own successful career.'

I was taken aback by her response. I could feel my face flushing red with anger. I tried to remain calm and reason with her.

'My so-called little operation provides a wonderful lifestyle for you and our children. And might I remind you that your much-lauded Cambridge degree is in law, Jennifer. Law, not economics! I was simply going to point out that the shockwaves from a collapse like this go all the way down the line, affecting everybody.'

'You mean straight to the kitchen,' she interrupted again. 'To me and all the other mums. What a joke.'

'Be that as it may, I'll forgive you your lack of financial knowledge.'

'Ha, you men, you got us into all this. You so-called experts. Your hero Bertie and now that gormless looking corpse that pretends to be leader, what's his name, Biffo? Hopeless, the lot of them.'

This was too much. 'Jennifer!' I shouted. 'That's outrageous. How dare you speak about good men like that. Ahern made this country great and now Cowen is trying to stabilise it after events over which he had no control have torpedoed all that was built up. He has to save the banks, otherwise we are all doomed.'

'Oh, brilliant. Throw more good money after bad. Make the people in the street pay. Have a bit of vision, why don't you? Think outside the square for once rather than coming up with the same tired old solutions.'

I moved in closer to her. I was getting angry. She was not only attacking my business acumen but the political party that I supported and which had served the country so well. I started to clench my fists.

She continued on. 'And now, after you've sat in your study and had a good cry like a baby, the family has to suffer.'

That was enough.

'Are you listening to me? Do you understand?' I hissed, moving up close to her, raising my hand.

'What?'

'Do you understand? I'm cutting your budget. Jennifer. Now, don't make me angry and force me to do something that we will both regret.' She looked at me blankly for a second and then stepped back. 'Do you understand?' I repeated.

'Yes, yes, I do, Stuart, I understand,' she said meekly.

'Good,' I said, dropping my hand. 'Just cut your cloth to suit, Jennifer, work within the budget that I set you and all will be fine.'

I left it at that and headed back to my study, moving slowly and deliberately, popping my head in the doorway of the lounge and saying a cheery 'Hi' to the boys, who were watching *The Karate Kid*.

As captain of the ship, I was angry that she should question my decision-making, but I was pleased that I had successfully put the mutiny down. 'Typical,' I thought, 'she not only knows nothing about high finance, but has no idea about real politics, as well.'

I did not raise the topic again, but I did notice that as part of the new regime, she started buying the cheaper brand of disposable razors and generic chocolate biscuits, so after a few weeks I quietly returned her allowance to its usual level and nothing further was said.

Things went back to normal on the home front. Or at least they did as far as I could see.

16

S olid and reliable as I was, there was always one chink in my armour. The computer. It was not my scene. That's a terrible admission from a man who worked in an industry that was so dependent on it. But I had sales duties to undertake. I had managerial responsibilities to uphold. I had executive powers to wield. And I had Doreen to do my paperwork for me.

Doreen was my long and faithful secretary, my grand support, my indestructible, ever-present, wise and all-knowing angel. She could do anything. Some said she ran my department, if not the whole company. I think that was a bit over-stated. But she certainly was invaluable, as I knew very little about modern technology.

Her role included translating all my paperwork and correspondence onto the computer. Call me a Luddite, but I was a fountain-pen man. I did all my work with a gold-plated Parker 61 Stratus with a 14 carat medium nib. I enjoyed the atmospheric sound it made as it moved across the page. I also wrote everything on yellow sheets of A4, the old-fashioned legal pad, giving it a sense of authority. Whether it was the draft of a letter, the rough calculations for a project or the general outline for a proposal, to me it looked 'real'. The figures had a profundity about them, the writing an air of elegance. At a meeting, people would be impressed when I'd pull out the pen, do some rough calculations on the yellow sheets and hand them around. Afterwards Doreen would magically turn it all into a neatly-typed printout.

Even my Letters to the Editor that I enjoyed writing and sending off to the newspapers, preferably *The Independent* or *The Irish Times*, I always did in long hand. It gave me a great feeling of satisfaction, putting my thoughts about the economy or a social issue down on quality paper with real ink, placing it in an envelope and mailing it from the letterbox at the end of our street.

One of my few forays into the computer world was to get Doreen to show me how to access the Stock Market for a daily update on the share prices. Later I got her to show me how to access an email account, for viewing purposes only. Personally, I did not like email. I felt that important messages could disappear amongst all the rubbish that filled up the inbox every morning. I had heard of sales being lost and projects coming unstuck because an email that had been sent in time to catch the deadline had gone unsighted. I did not necessarily want to be shown how to use email. I just wanted to check Jennifer's every now and then.

I did not think there was anything wrong with that. I felt that having the occasional discreet peek at his wife's correspondence was a reasonable thing for a husband to do, in order to see if there was any message or subject that might cause concern or require action. It was important, so that everyone could move forward together with no secrets or hidden agendas.

I was always pleased to discover that whenever I got into her email account, with the obvious password of

'Molly', Jennifer's notes to her friends and family seemed straightforward and contained nothing untoward. There were no recipients that I did not know or had not heard of.

But I hadn't counted on Facebook.

Oh, I'd heard about it all right. Some sort of friendship site where people swapped messages and photos about what they were up to. Putting little quotes online about what they were doing at that precise moment and that sort of thing. What they were cooking, what they were wearing and where they had partied. I remember one day how one of the girls in Accounts was having lunch at her desk and she showed me her screen as I walked past. 'Look at this, Mr Hoare,' she said, 'this is really cool.'

Cool? Some character had written that he was 'feeling good' and 'might go shopping'. Another said that this year he would 'not live in a campervan'. A third wrote, 'I am a fan of duct tape'. Riveting stuff.

I concluded it was the province of the young – teenagers and twenty-somethings with not many brains and too much time on their hands – and dismissed it out of hand. I didn't realise that people of all ages used it, including those in their 30s, 40s, 50s and even older. I did not know that Facebook groups were formed of people interested in specific subjects, campaigns and movements, the recruitment often being quite vigorous. Above all, I did not have a clue that it provided an online opportunity for two people to talk to each other, discreetly and privately, in order to develop a relationship.

What a fatal error on my part. Especially for a man working in an industry where errors were inexcusable, who admired Horatio Nelson for his tactical ability and who had been brought up by a father who insisted on always knowing what your enemy was up to.

What I also did not know was that Jennifer had set up a separate email to accept the Facebook 'alert' notes that members got advising them that something had happened on their account. Jennifer later tried to tell me that she had done that for convenience because so many emails were being sent telling her that a comment had been posted or a message had been sent or a photo had been tagged and so on. I eventually found out that that was a lie. She had all along been deliberately hiding the content of that Facebook email box from me.

One day I arrived home at 5.27 pm as usual, and the house was in typical order. The kids were doing their homework, Jennifer was cooking dinner and all seemed right with the world. But it wasn't. She had a somewhat distracted look; an edgy visage, one almost of fear. She was slightly pale and a little jittery.

She jumped when I entered the kitchen and her kiss on the cheek was even briefer than usual. I noticed she didn't really give me eye contact. But I'm an understanding man, lots of things can happen to a busy mother during the day. Getting kids in and out of cars, doing pick-ups, tramping from the butcher to the grocer, it can all build up. Besides, when I questioned her, she assured me she was all right. 'I'm fine,' she said, 'how was your day?'

'Oh, okay, I guess. Not much joy. You know, it's like Thailand, that sort of thing ..."

She reacted nervously to that. 'What did you say?'

'I said, things are like in Thailand.'

'Thailand? Why did you mention that?'

'Well, Thailand was one of the original Asian Tigers, along with Hong Kong, Taiwan and the others. It was the first to go down the gurgler and that, to me, sums up where Ireland is heading now. Why?'

'Oh, nothing, nothing,' she said, looking a little more relieved and going back to her cooking. I studied her for a moment, then poured myself a glass of wine and was about to pursue the matter – why would the mention of Thailand unsettle her? – when the Angelus finished on the television in the kitchen and the news theme began blaring. I wanted to watch the bulletin because I had heard around the traps that some sort of new bank was in the pipeline to take on the toxic loans that were dogging the Irish financial institutions and which hopefully might ease things. As the Taoiseach made his announcement, I ruminated on the situation the country was in. What a mess. Economic doom, the Celtic Tiger shot down, the future looking gloomy.

So, Jennifer's uneasiness passed from my mind. But later that evening she got short with the children when she put them to bed, which was something she rarely did. And although she was watching the programs she liked on the television, including a travel program about Asia, she said very little about it and retired early. The only other thing I noticed was that she made a point of turning the computer off. She didn't necessarily always do that, something which annoyed me because I felt that leaving a computer on was not only a waste of power but also could damage components, lose data or spark a fire.

I was not too good on some of those things, but from my view at the doorway of the study as she stood over the desk and pressed the mouse, what I saw disappearing as the computer shut down was the blue and white colours of a website. I deduce now, long after the event, that it must have been Facebook. It still grieves me to realise that when I asked her what it was, she stood there and blatantly told me it was a buying group and she was having a look to see if there were any bargains. Impressed with her thrift, I blithely moved on, suspecting and knowing nothing.

What an idiot I was, I should have pressed the issue, looked for the signs, did a little snooping around. But why should I? Things might have been bad in Ireland and terrible in Thailand, but at least the Hoare family was standing strong and united, wasn't it?

17

I never saw the next revelation coming at all. I never suspected for one minute that Jennifer, the person I had sworn my allegiance to by the banks of the Shannon on the eve of the summer solstice, would be anything other than faithful to me. I might have been a bit tough on her at times, but as I used to say whenever I made a decision that she did not agree with, 'It's for the good of the family, to keep us united and to protect our reputation.'

We had a successful marriage. We had a beautiful home. We had a lovely family. We had social currency and respect. Why would she want to jeopardize all that? I firmly believed that I was the captain of a good ship and that Jennifer and the children were an excellent crew despite she and Molly developing their own slightly mutinous group below decks. Surely no one in their right mind would want to send all that off course and condemn the whole thing to the bottom of the ocean?

She was the model wife. A bit scatty maybe, but a great mother to our children. Devoted to her own parents. And to mine, too. And as the years had rolled on, she never seemed to have deviated from that path. Never once did she give off a hint that something was going on. She maintained the same even-handed voice during my regular daily calls. She never used the house phone or her mobile for calls to strange numbers. I know that because I went through the bills with her every month and would immediately pick up on any new or unusual number. Her emails were clear and as far as I knew, Facebook was of little consequence.

I was so trusting that at one stage when Jennifer said, 'Can we get a laptop?' I acquiesced. She explained how the boys had a lot of homework and that having to share the home computer meant one of them might miss out and fall behind in his studies. That concerned me. She also pointed out that a laptop would be handy for her to help with the shopping and organising things. 'As well,' she said, 'one day soon I will be able to go back into the workforce, so it would be good for me to have my own computer.'

I had always made it clear that Jennifer was to never work again, even when the last of the kids started school. We had always agreed on our roles; I was the bread winner, she the home maker. But now, as things were getting tough, it didn't seem a bad idea to bring a little extra cash into the house. So I agreed, although rather than spend money on a new laptop, I brought home an old one from work which Doreen, my able secretary, assured me would function properly for years. It was perfect timing. I gave it to Jennifer for her birthday.

The laptop was easy enough to source as things were getting so tough at work that Derek and I had had to let a couple of salesmen go. The downsizing happened so quickly, I was soon able to bring another notebook home for the boys, too.

I started to realise that something was not right in the weeks after that evening when she had reacted so nervously when I mentioned Thailand. From that anxious moment on, a new Jennifer started to emerge. A slightly more self-confident Jennifer. Almost a disobedient Jennifer. She started chipping at me, firing back comments, ignoring my instructions. She started to display that oh-so-clever smile that her friend Wendy had perfected. And Wendy started to get more involved. Why, Wendy was even picking up the kids from school sometimes when Jennifer unaccountably found herself too late to be there. She started getting tardy about the meals, to the point of being careless about what the children were eating.

'Wait a minute,' I asked myself one day. 'What's all this about?'

Jennifer had never let the kids down, not once. I had, yes, I will freely admit that. Plenty of times I'd been late for concerts, missed soccer matches or tip-toed in at the back during the middle of a piano recital. Very often, at the most crucial of times when she needed my help most, I would not be there for her. Stuart Junior needs to be picked up from the dentist? I would be in an important meeting. Richard needs a lift to music? I would be at a business conference. Molly has to be taken to child care? 'Sorry, darling, I've got to drive over to Galway to stitch up a deal.'

I tried to participate as much as I could. But I was the money man, that was my job. Jennifer's job was to be the family woman. To stay home and look after the kids. We'd made an agreement that we would do it that way. Just as we had agreed to love, honour and be faithful to each other.

I was not the most sensitive of fellows, but after a while even I started to pick up the vibes from Jennifer. The nervousness, the belligerence, the cockiness, the tardiness. For a brief moment, I put it down to early menopause, but discarded that notion after I established that she didn't seem to be complaining of the other symptoms. Ironically, the subject of women's health came up when I found a packet of the pill in the bathroom, something she had not used for years, much to my obvious annoyance.

'What are these doing here?' I said. 'I know we hardly make love anymore. But when we do, you make me wear a condom. So, what's going on?'

She looked embarrassed and rather ruffled. She quickly and quietly took the packet out of my hand and regained her compsoure. 'I've been having women's troubles, darling,' she said blithely. 'Heavy bleeding. The doctor prescribed these to see if it will help.'

That threw me a bit. 'Are you all right?' I said.

'I'll be fine. We'll see how these work.'

I stared at her for a while, figured that that was fair enough and decided it would be best to leave an intimate matter like that alone.

However, from then on I began to quietly observe that Jennifer would become especially agitated, evasive and lose focus for three days in succession once a month. Always during the week, never the weekend. There appeared to be some sort of sequence, one which simply could not be put down to her menstrual cycle, the phases of the moon or even some of her more bizarre New Age theories.

Short of fronting her directly, I was struggling to find an answer, until one day, Doreen inadvertently provided the goods. Just before she was leaving work she said to me, 'I'm having dinner with someone special tonight.'

'Oh yes?' I said, a little surprised. This was indeed a turn up for the books. Doreen was only a couple of years younger than me, had never been married and had never indicated she was seeking a partner.

'I met someone on Facebook,' she said chirpily.

I looked at her stupidly. 'Doreen, with respect, what are you doing on something like that at your age? Isn't that for the young?'

'Oh, no, no,' she enthused. 'All sorts of people use it. Young, old, friends, family, husbands, wives, lovers …'

'Lovers?'

'Yes, you don't have to make everything public, you know. You can talk discreetly, set up a whole romance, have a little tryst and no one will know.'

She giggled and looked to the heavens. 'Now that my poor dear mother has departed after years of sufferin' and I have the house to myself and all the time in the world, it's my chance for a bit of fun.'

I stared at her lamely as she picked up her coat and headed for the door. 'I'll let you know how I get on,' she said cheerily. I watched as she disappeared down the corridor. Then I looked down at her computer, then back at her receding figure and then at the computer again. I began to think, to link things together, to work elements through. Facebook. Discreet conversations. Lovers. I walked back into my own office, circled my desk a couple of times and then came back. Tentatively, I touched the space bar. Bingo. In her haste to meet her potential paramour, Doreen had not turned the computer off. The screen lit up to reveal the home page of Facebook. I tapped in Jennifer's email – the new one, the Gmail one that I had spotted on her laptop screen one night – and tried 'Molly' for the password.

The Facebook Home Page of Jennifer Hoare came up.

And so did he.

Right underneath her profile photo were pictures of six of Jennifer's friends. I knew the other five, including of course Karena and that damn Wendy. But not the sixth. Not him. Not this fellow. Not this, what's his name, let me see now? Tom.

I looked around the page using my limited skills with the mouse, flicking the cursor all over the place, scrolling things up and down, following the discussions between Jennifer and others – and him – on the screen. A lot of it was rubbish, but the more I read, the more I increasingly felt anxious, alarmed and finally sick to the stomach. You could tell from the energy and intimacy of the public dialogue between the two of them that something was going on. And if that was what they were letting anybody read, then God knows what they were saying to each other in private. Or, for that matter, doing.

I anxiously clicked at the buttons on the page with a clammy hand. Somehow, even with my computer incompetency, his profile came up and I read it quickly. I could see already from the picture what his genetics were. He was not pure Anglo Saxon, that was for sure. The colour of his skin and shape of his eyes attested to that. Now I read all about his background, where he lived, what he did for a job and some of his philosophical views on life. Ah-ha! Look at this. His mother was Thai! No wonder Jennifer went to water when I mentioned Thailand in the kitchen one night.

And there was the clincher. A little note at the bottom. 'Just to remind everybody I will be in Dublin from the 21st to the 23rd next month, as usual.'

I hastily cast my eyes around Doreen's well-organised desk and snatched up the calendar. My fingers were shaking as I flipped it over to the next month. The 21st to the 23rd. There it was. Three days in the middle of the week. The sort of time sequence each month when Jennifer would get unsettled. Just as I had worked out.

I have never been so furious, so angry, so riven with rage since that day at school when I snapped after years of being treated so badly by the in-house bullies. It was a level of anger that I had never attained since, a feeling that I had always successfully subsumed when the pressure was on. But not this time. I could feel my cheeks burning with indignation.

I squeezed the calendar so hard that all the blood drained from my hand. I hurled it against the wall. I stepped back, stared at the smiling face on the screen and yelled. 'Arrrgggghhh!'

The cry of anguish and anger reverberated through the empty building.

My God! My wife was having an affair! With some character called Tom. A half-Asian Buddhist drummer living in some dive in the East End of London.

LOVER, HUSBAND, FATHER, MONSTER

18

I am not called Stu for nothing. I stewed.

I stewed and stewed every minute of every day over the terrible prospect that my wife was having an affair.

I stewed over it in the car on the way to work, I stewed over it all day at my office, I stewed over it in the car on the way home. I stewed over it in meetings, while standing in the ATM queue, even while sitting by the lake in the park eating my lunch-time sandwiches and solemnly watching the ducks.

Two conflicting arguments banged away in my brain. On the one hand, I was certain the bitch was doing it. I wanted to confront her there and then. Question her, interrogate her, get the story out of her. Use force if I had to. What a situation. Here was some jumped up little drummer having sex with my wife while I was going through endless periods of frustration or having to recourse to the demeaning solution of self gratification through fantasy. She was not going to get away with it. I fumed every time I thought about it.

On the other hand, I had no real proof. I was only guessing, surmising, extrapolating a devastating conclusion from a few scrappy comments I had seen on Facebook. What if I was wrong? What if they were just friends having a chat? What if I rushed in, starting shooting first and asking questions later, only to discover it was all innocent and above board? Then the whole thing would have blown up in my face. I would have broken the bond between Jennifer and me, making myself look very foolish in the process.

'Stuart,' I would say to myself, 'you've constructed the worst possible scenario out of nothing.' It was quite possible. Even though I was from the 'old school', I had come to appreciate that the concepts of friendship, partnership and marriage had changed so radically that things were no longer clear cut. You were once able to say, 'This is my wife, now hands off,' and people would respect that. But nowadays, people drift in and out of relationships, they become enamored with someone via all these modern technological devices, cyber-mating or something I think it is called, and nothing is ever set in stone or follows the old norms. You hear a couple explain, 'We've split up, but we're still good friends.' That is rubbish as far as I am concerned; ex-lovers cannot retain their friendship. Once it's over, it's over and they should never go near one another ever again. But in our brave new world, people believe that to end a relationship, take the sex out of it, and yet somehow remain firm friends is a tenable view.

So I stewed over both sides of the argument, especially at home. And particularly when Jennifer darted around the kitchen preparing meals, humming a little tune to herself. Or when she sat next to me in the lounge with the television guide in her hand asking me what I wanted to watch. Or when she greeted me with, 'How was your day?'

'How was my day?' I used to think to myself. 'How was my day, you ask? Fantastic, couldn't have been better. Here I am, up to my arse in work, trying to find ways to salvage the thousands we've lost while you're having it off with a layabout Asian percussionist. Great! Couldn't be better.'

Then I used to think, 'Hang on, it would be crazy saying that. Even if I am right, I'm just focusing on money. There's more to that than this. What about loyalty to each other? What about trust? What about being devoted to the family unit? Maybe those things don't mean much to her anymore.'

I would consider trying the placatory technique. I would imagine how I would put it: 'Darling, I realise that I have not been the best of husbands. I know our relationship has suffered, a lot of it being my fault through my devotion to work and rigid old-fashioned principles. I understand how you could be tempted to fall into the arms of someone else – not that I am saying you have, of course – but surely we can fix things before they get too bad?'

I used to think about how others would have approached it. The ice cool Derek, my business partner, would have calmly said, 'I've worked out exactly what's going on, I'm walking out, staying at a hotel, and a letter from my solicitor will be delivered to you in the morning.'

Buchanan would have given his wife the biggest bollocking, called her a 'feckin' slut,' reduced her to tears, then added that it was probably as much his fault as hers, opened a bottle of wine and tried to get her up to the bedroom.

But most of the time, I just seethed. I wanted to confront Jennifer, to say something, to elicit a response from her and gauge my next move based on what she said and, equally importantly, how she said it. Angry and furious as I was, I knew I really only had one shot at this and I used to think about every possible option as I paced up and down the lounge room late at night. I wanted answers, explanations, but I did not want to mess it up, to wreck everything, to destroy the lot. I had to be patient. As my father used to say about resolving issues, 'Be like an Army Court Martial, son. First, work out the result you want, and then set up the terms of reference to get it.'

I briefly thought about seeking more of Dad's wise counsel. But the Alzheimer's had chewed out his brain and he would have contributed little. My mother would have been of limited help, too, as she was now fully pre-occupied with Dad's illness. Besides, she and Jennifer had developed a very close relationship over the years and she adored the kids. I was sure she would have hated to see the family unit split, no matter how unpalatable the situation. How wrong that thinking proved to be.

I certainly did not want to consult Jennifer's family, either. They had a love/hate relationship with me at the best of times and the majority vote would have come down on her side, especially amongst her brothers. The general consensus, particularly endorsed by her father Seamus and her closest brother Kevin, would have been that I had been a poor choice in the first place and who could blame her for getting a bit of excitement on the side? Besides, no matter who I would have carefully picked out from her family for a discreet discussion sworn to secrecy, the story would have spread around that sprawling, brawling bunch of ignorant Micks like wildfire.

There was only one way to find out. I hired a private detective.

Actually, he surprised me. I thought he would be wearing a pin-stripe, double-breasted suit and a grey Fedora hat, ceaselessly igniting cigarettes from a silver lighter that clanged loudly every time he shut it. But he was an ordinary man in ordinary clothes who could slip in and out of any crowd unnoticed. 'That's the name of the game,' he said.

He was very good at it, too, and the fifteen hundred euro that he charged, which I quietly slipped into the sundries column of the firm's monthly accounts, was well worth it. Distressing, but worth it. A picture of this Tom character entering a hotel in Dublin, followed by a snap of Jennifer entering a few minutes later. The third print, of them later fondly farewelling each other on the front steps, was enough to convince me. The closeness, the intimacy and the joy shown by their body language said it all. They had rekindled more than a friendship.

'I've got another shot here, taken with a long lens straight into the hotel window,' the investigator said, peering into a large envelope. 'It doesn't show them actually doing it, but you can see they're getting well prepared. I observed them for a little while, until the point where even I have to show a bit of discretion. Some sort of dance, preparing for intercourse, like a ritual.'

I held up my hands, palms out, and shook my head. Curious as I was, I declined to see it. I'd seen plenty and was outraged enough as it was.

That night when I came home from work, looked around and observed the state of the house, I knew I had to make a stand. Dinner had not been prepared, the place was in semi darkness, there was rubbish and toys and papers all over the place, the kids were all staring hypnotically at the television and Jennifer was in the study tapping away furiously on the laptop.

I pulled the photos out of my brief case, calmly walked into the room, immediately recognised from the blue and white page that she was on Facebook, strode up, grabbed the screen of the laptop and slammed it down. She only saw me loom over her at the last second and barely got her fingers out of the way as the lid hit the keyboard. She looked up at me, shocked. I think she knew what was coming, but was trying to act innocent.

'Stuart! What's the matter?'

I held back for as long as I could, staring straight into her eyes. The longer I sustained the silence, the more uncomfortable she became. I wanted her to think that the worst was going to happen – because it was about to.

Finally, I leaned right into her face, and spoke very slowly.

'Tell me about Tom,' I hissed.

'Who? How did you …?' she gulped, before regaining a little composure. I could see her Irish Catholic butter-wouldn't-melt-in-its-mouth rat cunning working over time. 'Oh, why, Tom, he's just an old friend, from Cambridge days,' she said chirpily.

'And he's reappeared out of the blue, just like that?' I said cynically.

'Yes.'

'On the computer?'

'Yes, that's what happens on Facebook,' she said, nodding nervously towards the laptop. 'Friends from the past spot your name and get in touch. It happens all the time.'

I waited. She looked up at me for a moment and then looked down at the closed laptop again.

'And ..?' I said.

'And what?' she said, still looking down.

'What sort of friend is he?'

She clasped her hands in her lap and bowed her head further. When she replied, I could barely hear her.

'A good friend,' she whispered.

'How good?'

There was a long moment's hesitation.

'Just good friends, that's all,' she whispered.

I pulled the computer away from her and with both hands, lifted it high above my head and smashed it down on the corner of the antique hardwood desk. The thwack made her jump.

'Stuart!'

I leaned close into her face again. 'You're not telling the truth.'

'I am, I am! We're just friends from the past. His mother is from Thailand.'

'Oh, Thailand! Ah, now things are starting to become clearer. I mentioned Thailand in the kitchen one night and you nearly had a fit.'

She looked up, anxiously. 'Well ... there's the Buddhist thing ... we were both at Cambridge together, and after ...'

'After?'

'After, um, after ... a while, we lost touch.'

'But now you're back, as you so nicely put it, in touch, huh?'

'We're just friends! On Facebook.'

I slammed the notebook hard down on the desk again. A memory stick in a side port flew off with such force it bounced across the floor into the corner. The screen had started to fragment.

'You're more than friends, aren't you? Hey? More than friends?'

I hit the notebook down on the table again. Bang! The sound reverberated through the house. 'You've been seeing him!'

'No! No! I swear. Stuart, you're scaring me. There's nothing to this, we just talk on Facebook that's all.'

'Don't give me that crap.'

'Honest! We just chat on the computer. I haven't seen him. I swear!'

I threw the three photos down on the desk. 'Oh, yes?' I said. She gasped as I spread them out in front of her. Him going into the hotel. Her going into the hotel. The pair of them kissing as they left the hotel.

Her head jolted back in shock, her eyes began to glisten with tears, her bottom lip began to quiver.

'Well?' I continued. 'This is a nice little family photo album, isn't it? Huh? You say you haven't seen him, but there he is, in this picture. And there is you in that picture. Oh, and look at this, there you are in this one, together! He looks more than a friend in these, doesn't he? He looks very much part of the scene.'

'All right. Okay. We met just once, in the city, just to catch up. That's all. Nowhere else. There's nothing …'

Before she could finish, a third voice intervened.

'Mummy …' We both looked around. It was a tiny, subdued voice, coming from the doorway. The three kids had left the television and had come over to see what was happening, concerned and anxious.

'Mummy,' continued Stuart Junior, his voice a whisper. 'Does Daddy mean the man that was here one day when I got sick and stayed home from school ..?'

19

It was a gut-wrenching, soul-destroying statement that Stuart Junior had so innocently uttered. The moment he mentioned 'the man' who had been in the house on the day he was ill, the memory started flooding back to me. How I had come back one afternoon to pick up some important papers that I had forgotten when I'd left home that morning. How I had stopped to talk to Pete the postman in the driveway. And how, when I had let myself in, Jennifer was washing up several dishes, including two coffee cups. This had seemed odd and when I questioned her, she made some excuse about her Mam being over for a chat that day. Normally I would have checked up on it, but I was so pre-occupied with the Tallaght disaster that I let it go. I should have discreetly asked her mother later whether she had been at our place that day or not.

Now, out of the mouth of an unknowing child, it was all becoming clear to me. That he – this monster, this home-wrecker, this Tom – was not only liaising with my wife in hotels but had been in our house, too! Why, that day that I had turned up unexpectedly, he must have been only a few metres away, hiding in another room while I was standing there chatting to my wife. The person who I loved, worshipped and trusted.

My mind started racing. What else had there been? Why, yes, of course. He was probably also there that time I rang Jennifer's mobile and she sounded quite flustered when she answered. She passed it off as being excited about one of the kids having had some success at school. But, my God, I now realised that she was probably in bed with him when she answered the phone. That's why she was so breathless and not making much sense. They had just had sex. He was lying next to her while I was talking to her on the phone. He would have had his dirty little drummer hands all over her, playing with her, smirking while she blatantly told me lies. The thought of that inflamed my brain.

Barely able to contain my anger, I remained calm enough to give the kids five euro and tell them to go down to the village to get an ice cream. Something like that, I can't exactly remember, anything to get them out of the way. 'Mummy and Daddy have something to talk about,' I said evenly.

I was livid, almost out of control. When the front door latch clicked, I leaned right into Jennifer's face and hissed:

'So, he *has* been here, then?'

'Ah …' She dropped her head.

'Don't fucking lie to me, Jennifer!'

'Yes,' she whispered finally. 'Yes, he has.'

I wanted to explode. I wanted to hit her. I wanted to go and find the little bastard and kill him. But I also wanted to ask two more questions, get two more pieces of information, to confirm the depth of her infidelity.

'Be very careful about how you answer this next question, Jennifer. I will ask you just once. Did you have sex here, in this house?'

There was a long silence. Her head stayed down. 'Huh?' I barked. 'Answer me! Did you screw him here, in our house? The home we have built up together?'

After a few more seconds, she nodded her head imperceptibly and whispered, 'Yes.'

I stepped back, blinked and shook my head. I took a deep breath and leaned down close to her face again.

'So, was it in our bed? Hey? Did you fuck him in our bed?'

There was a long, long pause, as she struggled for breath. 'Yes,' she finally whispered. 'In our bed.'

'God damn it! You fucking slut!'

That was all I needed to hear. The Court Martial had sat. All admissions had been tendered. The defendant was guilty as charged. Sullying the matrimonial home with lust. Punishment was to be delivered. I punched her in the ribs. It was short, it was sharp, it was sweet. It was brutal. All those years of martial arts training melded into one stunning blow. My fist barely moved an inch, yet it connected with such force that I could hear the ribs crack as she doubled over in pain. I had not felt such a surge of unbridled power or such a release of deeply repressed anger since the day I snapped in the boarding school yard and pole-axed the college bully. And just like that day all those years before, once the flood gates were open, nothing was going to stop me. As Jennifer let out a piercing scream of pain, I punched her again, and again, and again, grabbing her by the hair with my free hand and pulling her face up towards me.

'You bitch,' I screamed. 'You fucking little bitch. So that's all you think of our marriage. Huh?'

She clutched at her ribs with her right hand and clawed for breath, slowly bringing her left hand up to her face to wipe her dripping nose with her sleeve. She dropped her head again, sobbing. 'Answer me, you slut!' I shouted, pushing my fist up close to her face. 'Fucking answer me or I'll ruin that pretty face forever!' At the sight of my raised fist, she began mumbling, incoherently at first, stumbling and mumbling and catching her breath, trying to get some words out. And slowly, piece by piece, little by little, her shoulders hunched and shaking, her head bowed so low it was almost touching the damaged noteboook keyboard, her eyes streaming with tears and her nose running, Jennifer told me all.

In little more than a whisper, with me prodding here every now and then and saying, 'Yes, and then what?', she related how she had studied with this Tom fellow in Cambridge, how they had been drawn together by Buddhism, how they had become great friends, and then, yes, how they had become lovers. How, with the energetic naivety of youth, they had tried to save the world by endeavouring to stop the French from testing their nuclear weapons in the Pacific. How his drumming skills had distracted him from his studies. How their romance, like many other glorious loves across the centuries, had dramatically collapsed and they had gone their own separate ways. How they had stayed totally apart, out of all communication, for twenty years or so until they were drawn back together again by a fluke of technology. Faceook. That damn Facebook.

Most of it I could handle. After all, Jennifer and I had not met each other until I was thirty-eight and she was thirty-one. You would have to be pretty naive if you thought that a person of that age had not experienced at least some real life adventures by then. Even someone from conservative little Ireland and from a super-protective family such as hers. You couldn't assume that she had spent her entire life wrapped in cotton-wool and had not ventured out into the real world and tasted its various delights including, of course, sex. Especially a woman as beautiful, vivacious and outgoing as Jennifer. She simply must have had a lover or lovers somewhere along the line. I'm not entirely worldly-wise but I'm not totally stupid either.

In our early days across the dinner table, she had obviously told me about her childhood and schooling, her university life, her career and some of the more personal, intimate background, including having had 'a couple of boyfriends.' But I now realised that I had been fed the sanitized version, one that in retrospect reeked of antiseptic that my lovelorn nostrils had not detected or had not wanted to detect. She had never told me about Tommy, now all grown up and known as Tom. Never once mentioned his name.

'Jennifer,' I said, as she finished her explanation and her voice trailed off, 'I have another question.'

There was another long pause. I grabbed her by the hair and yanked her head around to make sure she was facing me.

'You don't love this little drummer boy, do you?'

She took a deep breath, wincing in pain, and looked straight at me.

'Jennifer? You don't do you?' I demanded, shaking her head. 'You can't possibly? Not after what he did to you? Not after all we have shared together and built up?'

She peered into my eyes; she began to focus properly. She cleared her throat and her voice became a little stronger.

'Yes, I do.'

God damn! I pulled her hair as hard as I could, angrily spinning her head around in circles three, maybe four, times before letting go. I could feel a clump of her once radiant auburn crowning glory come away in my hands. Her head slumped forward. Her sobbing echoed through the room. I stepped back from her and readied my fist again. I figured it was about time those juicy lips of hers were made a bit fatter. I was about to grab her by the hair again and punch her in the face, when my eye caught the framed picture of our wedding on the sideboard behind her. She looked stunning on that night in her palest of green dresses. 'No, wait,' I thought to myself, 'don't smash up that beautiful face. People will notice.' Instead, I delivered another hard blow to the kidney area.

As she screamed and slumped forward in pain, gasping for breath, I concluded there was something better that I could do. Destroy their means of communication. Before her very eyes.

I unclenched my fist, picked up the laptop, raised it above my head, and smashed it once more on the solid hardwood table. I did it again. And again and again. It started to break into bits, the screen coming off and falling onto the wooden floor with a clatter as she shielded her eyes and continued whimpering, jumping involuntarily every time it banged on the table.

I thumped it again and again until, exhausted, I could do it no more. Then I picked up the broken screen, staggered over to the window, opened it, and threw the bits and pieces out into the garden. Worn out by the exertion, I slumped in a chair in the corner, trying to regain my breath, my strength and my composure.

The sobbing continued for a few moments. Then she looked up, took a deep breath, and spoke quietly, albeit with some force.

'At least there was a real man in the bed,' she said.

'What?' I said. It was difficult to hear her as I tried to catch my breath. 'What did you just say?'

'I said,' she hissed angrily, standing up, bent over, clutching her ribs, 'at least there was a real man in the bed.' She picked up a shard of the broken laptop, summoned all her strength and, screaming in agony, hurled it at me. I ducked at the last second as it whizzed by and smashed into the wall. 'There hasn't been one in it for years,' she gasped as she struggled out of the room and headed for the stairs.

'Well, well, well,' I thought, 'there's no denying the guts of a feisty little Irish red-head. Down and out on the mat, but still cocky enough to stand up and give a bit of lip. No wonder they're always in fights.' I started to pull myself out of the chair to chase her, but I could hardly move, I was so emotionally and physically drained. She had half-crawled, half-walked up to the landing before I could get my aching body shifting with any speed. By the time I got some traction and climbed a few steps, she had staggered into the bathroom, slammed the door and locked it. I could hear her coughing and gasping for breath as she began manhandling a chest of antique drawers, the one we used to store towels. There was a scraping sound as it was dragged across the tiles and a thump as it was wedged hard up against the door. If I was fresh and fit, I reckoned I could have run right through it and burst inside. But I was exhausted. I tried to crash it a couple of times with my shoulder, to no avail. 'You slut,' I screamed, banging on the door, before going back down stairs, rubbing my shoulder as I went. I picked up the keyboard of the dismembered laptop, went back up the stairs to the landing and hurled it at the bathroom door. 'There you go, princess,' I shouted as it bounced off the door and landed on the floor. 'See if you can chat to the little prick now!'

I went downstairs and slumped in the chair. 'What a fool,' I thought. 'What an idiot I've been. I thought she loved me but now I know what I suspected was true all along. I was just the meal ticket, the bunny that appeared on the horizon when she thought all her hopes of marriage and children were gone. Last chance Stu. That was me. The provider of the cash, the sperm and the security. And once I'd done my job, she figured it was party time.'

After a while, I began to regain my strength, my mind began to clear and I worked out what I had to do. Wait. Just wait. She would have to come out of there some time and I could then reason with her, try and make her see what she had done, tell her to give up this nonsense and return things to the way they were.

That's it, I would wait. I sat in the chair, staring at the wedding photo on the other side of the room. Then my mobile rang. It was Buchanan, his normally cheery voice sounding exceptionally stressed. 'Stu, Stu, more problems at Tallaght,' he said. 'Some bastard is suing us. Can I meet you in the pub in fifteen, we need to talk.'

I let out a deep sigh. This was all I needed. More difficulties with that damn building project. Why, oh why, didn't I just stick to insurance? 'Sure, okay,' I said. 'In fifteen.'

The meeting only added to my stress; the situation was getting worse. When I returned that night, the boys were watching television but Jennifer was nowhere to be seen. She had taken Molly with her and gone over to her mother's. Any chance to try and reason with her had evaporated. We had moved into very dangerous territory.

20

I n the cool light of the next day, I began to think things through. 'Let's look at this carefully,' I thought. 'We are both adults. We are living under the same roof. We've built a lot up together. We both have responsibilities, particularly shared ones. There are three other very important people involved – young, innocent ones – plus the extended family.'

Even though I was furious, it made sense not to do something really silly over this one situation and throw everything away. So after all the tears and the admissions and the punching and the screaming and the throwing and the smashing had subsided, we met, we talked and we settled into a nice, simple compromise: I forbade her to see Tom again and she agreed that she wouldn't.

Okay, maybe that is not quite a compromise, more an instruction, a direct order from the captain on the bridge. Jennifer was the perpetrator and I was the humiliated, innocent and aggrieved party. End of story.

Admittedly it took me a while to get her to see the wisdom of my decision. Only consideration of the likely impact on our children made her see sense. 'Think about the kids,' I said. 'Look what happened to your brother's family after he got caught with his secretary.' That seemed to hit home. Following Patrick's indiscretion on his phantom golf trip to Galway, Kathy had been forced to go back to her home town of Tipperary and live the life of the single mother in a down-market flat. The kids, particularly the two in the sensitive early teenage stage, lost all interest in school and drifted into drugs, booze and strife. 'Besides, Jennifer,' I added, 'let me make it quite clear. If you go off with this Tom character, you will never see your children again. Never! Do you understand? Never!'

So, after some moody silence, Jennifer agreed to what I proposed and over the next few weeks life returned to something approaching normal. I was pleased that we had reached some sort of detente because things were really starting to bite at work. Money was even harder to come by and policies were not being renewed; with some clients, not even on their cars. When a recession hits, people start cutting corners and taking risks. Insurance is often one of the first aspects of their life that they abandon. We had to let more staff go and the Tallaght project had become a mess. We were one of the lucky ones in that the actual shells of the buildings had got to lock-up stage. But it was a very sad sight to see, with the rooms all empty, the wind whistling across the barren plaza and the tags of the graffiti louts all over the walls.

Angered by these so-called artistic endeavours of the disaffected youth, I dashed off a letter one day to *The Independent* proposing that anyone caught in the possession of a bag of those infernal spray cans should be immediately jailed for three months, no questions asked, no quarter given. Naturally enough, many of the published replies in the following days were from civil libertarian types castigating me for such a provocative proposal. But a reader from Sandyford, God bless him, said that I should stand in the next election on a law and order ticket and I would be guaranteed success.

Out of all this, the pressure was really on me and Derek to find new clients to keep the business afloat. But despite having to work even harder and trying to cope with the stress of it all, I still remained vigilant about Jennifer's movements. My trust had been broken once and it was going to take a lot of hard work on her behalf to go even a little way to restoring it.

I was starting to feel somewhat calmer during the following two months – particularly the timeframe when I knew that that loathsome little individual Tom would be in Dublin to record his tacky television program. It had some ridiculous name like *Who? When? What?* or something. But from what I could see, instead of chasing after Tom at that time, like she had done before, Jennifer stayed around the house. She seemed to be calm and content and not trying to get in touch with him. That was going to be pretty hard for her, anyway. I had not replaced the notebook that I had smashed and I had also banned her from using both the other laptop and the home computer to access Facebook. Regular checks, including rigorous examination of every number on the phone bills, convinced me that she was sticking to her promise.

But in the third month, when I knew Tom would be back in Dublin again, things began to go awry. Throughout the Thursday, usually his last day in town for the recording, I could not contact Jennifer. She did not answer the home phone for my regular calls and her mobile was switched off. I rang a few of her friends, even that damned Wendy, who I hated talking to at the best of times, but they all said they knew nothing of her whereabouts. At least, that is what they claimed.

When I got home Jennifer said she had been out shopping for an outfit for Molly but had struggled to find something that would fit her because she was so tiny. More expense on clothes! And, she explained, her mobile battery was flat, and the house phone connection had been knocked out accidentally by the vacuum cleaner when she was cleaning that morning. And so on, and so on. Yeah, yeah, I had enough problems to worry about without being concerned with that sort of rubbish.

On the Friday, she was jumpy and anxious and I began to suspect something was up. I would have questioned her that evening but I had to go down to the church for an important committee meeting, which went on much longer than expected, and when I got home she was asleep.

On the Saturday, I followed my usual routine of rising early and taking the two boys with me to my weekly golf game, where they could caddy for me while I played and then practice a few pitches and putts under my direction after the match. When we came home from the course and entered the front door, to my amazement I was greeted not by my wife but my mother!

With a concerned look on her face, she pushed the boys into the lounge room, shut the door behind them, and then ushered me into the parlour on the other side of the hallway. She closed that door behind her and stared at me, shaking her head from side to side.

'Mum!' I said, 'what's going on? Is something wrong with Jennifer? With Molly?'

She looked straight at me with a strength and firmness I had never seen in her eyes before. 'It's the violence, Stuart,' she said. 'I put up with it from your father for years and I don't want Jennifer to have to suffer it like I did.'

I froze. She continued to stare straight at me. I didn't know which revelation shocked me more. That my father had been violent to her, something I had certainly never noticed in all the time I was at home – well, not anything that I would consider untoward – or that she considered my approach to Jennifer just as unacceptable.

'Mum, I never knew.'

'It happened,' she said. 'He used to try and pass it off as a result of his war days. But it was more than that. It was his way of controlling me. It wouldn't have mattered if he had been in the army or not, he still would have done it anyway.'

'But, Mum, me and Jennifer, I've never laid ...'

'Don't!' she said, holding her hand up and stopping me. 'Don't lie to me, Stuart, I'm your mother. Don't try and defend yourself. She's shown me the bruises around the ribs, the bits of her pretty hair pulled out, the marks on her back. And when I was here one day and saw the pieces of that computer thing all over the garden and asked the kids what was going on, that was it.'

I could feel the anger welling in me. My ship was now under serious threat. Jennifer, my mutinous first mate, had been blabbing to everyone; even the children were proving a security risk.

'So, what's going on, then?' I said. 'What's this all about?'

'Stuart, she wants to be free of you. She's going to London to live with Tom.'

'Bullshit!'

'Stuart, please don't swear in front of me like that.'

'There is no fucking way my wife is leaving me and her children to go and live with that little prick.'

'She's not leaving all of the kids. She's taking Molly with her.'

I stepped back, my head spinning.

'What? Like hell she is! I'll soon sort this out.' I went to push past Mum and head for the door, but she stood firmly in front of me.

'Stuart,' she said resolutely. 'Just listen. You can see Jennifer in a minute, and tell her whatever you want, but please hear what I have to say first. You can't blame her for wanting a new life.'

'New life? She went off and …'

'No, no, wait, wait. She might have been unfaithful, but …'

'She certainly was!'

' … but that was after the event, Stuart. Did she ever bash you? No. Did she pull your hair out in clumps? No. Did she ridicule you in front of people, or insist on what clothes you wore, or check up on your every move, or complain when the meal was not right, or make sarcastic comments about the house-keeping? No, she didn't. She didn't do any of those things, Stuart, you did. *You* were the one who made *her* life miserable!

'I, ah …'

'And that is something that a mother is not proud to say about her son, I can tell you.'

'Oh, mum, I didn't mean …'

'You may not have meant it, Stuart, but it happened. You did it. Look, I know she has done a terrible thing to you and I know you are hurt and you feel betrayed.'

'I've got every right to feel betrayed!'

'But you instigated this, Stuart. You set up the division. You split her and Molly away from you.'

'I, ah …' I tried to respond, but nothing came out. I felt confused, hurt, deflated. Mum put her hand up and lightly touched my cheek.

'Look at it this way. You will still have the boys. That's a good thing. You love them and they love you. And Mary and I will help you with them. We'll make sure you get plenty of support with meals and pick-ups and all that sort of thing. You'll still be able to run the business and they will get on with their education and sport and whatever else they want to do in life.'

'Well, I guess …'

'Stuart, it will take all the sting out of the situation. All the heat and the argument and the unhappiness. I know this is hurting you now, but it will be best in the long run. You never know, she might even come back home to you one day.'

'If and when she returns to her senses,' I replied flatly.

'That's right! Come with me now, she's in the lounge. Come and say goodbye and wish her well and just let things rest. It's for the best.'

I looked down at Mum. She stared straight back at me, her soft blue eyes pleading, begging me to follow her wishes.

'Please, Stuart?'

'Okay,' I mumbled, 'okay.'

She looked relieved, gave a wan smile, grabbed me by the hand and led me out of the room. Still a little stunned, I obediently traipsed behind her as she crossed the hallway, opened the lounge room door and led me in. And there they all were. A blur of faces and bodies, variously sitting stiffly or standing awkwardly around the room, waiting in ambush. A whole group of them, family and friends, the stand-outs being Jennifer's mum, Mary,

165

and her brother, Kevin, no doubt to provide a bit of muscle if things turned nasty. Perhaps he had heard about my judo triumph in Cork all those years ago.

I surveyed them all and took a deep breath. 'Ah, a welcoming committee,' I said, trying to break the ice.

Jennifer was at centre stage. Her skin was pale and tightly drawn and she was nervous, but I could see she was determined to make a stand.

'I've booked a flight to London,' she said.

'So I understand,' I replied. 'Mum told me.'

'I'm going with Tom.'

It suddenly dawned on me that the squeamish little bastard was standing opposite me. A fair distance away, I might point out. My mother might have told me some home truths and calmed me down and softened me up for this moment, but the mention of his name and the sight of him fired me up again. I started to move towards him. 'I'm gonna knock your block off,' I yelled. I reckoned I could have, too. He was much tinier than I had envisaged. 'You fucking little prick. She's my wife, not yours.'

You could hear the collective intake of breath, the murmurs of shock as I strode across the room, only to be blocked by Kevin. He had quickly moved across to stand between me and Tom. He folded his arms, set his jaw firmly and adopted a wide stance. It appeared he had acquired a few basic combat techniques while he'd been losing my money on the race track. I pushed him in the chest, but he remained solid.

'Kevin, my fight is not with you,' I hissed. 'Out of my way.'

'No can do, Stuart,' he said.

'Kevin, I do not want to have to hurt you.'

'Stuart,' came a pleading voice. It was Jennifer. 'Please do not make a scene.'

'A scene!' I said, turning around to look at her. 'Me, make a scene, for Christ's sake? You're the one that has set the scene, wrecking our family, pulling our lives apart.'

'Stuart, you started it all when you began to control me. To run my life, to insist that everything be done your way.'

'Jennifer, I was only doing the best for the family. To keep things on an even keel. You know how scatty you can get.'

'Scatty? Ha! Listen, I ran that house perfectly, all day every day, and raised three healthy, happy little kids, and all you did was turn up, eat, drink whiskey and whinge. If I ever appeared scatty it was my way of trying to be happy and making the best of the miserable life you chained me to.'

'Well, that's marriage for you, Jennifer. That's what it's all about. You have your ups and downs, your good days and your bad days. And you work through the bad stuff. You don't just suddenly walk out and end it all.'

'Well, I am. I've made up my mind. I've had enough of the pain and the misery and the beatings, and I'm going. Molly's coming with me and the boys can stay with you.'

I looked around the room. There were heads quietly nodding in assent everywhere.

She went on, spouting enthusiastically about how Junior and Rich would be happier and more secure with me, continuing to live in the same house, going to the same school, having the same friends, all that sort of stuff.

'And Molly will be better off with me,' she concluded. I looked across the room to see Tom step aside and reveal Molly who, up until now, had been standing behind him. My little girl took the loathsome individual's hand and looked up at me with a sad expression on her face, her little green eyes looking melancholy and confused.

'But, she's my daughter, too. You can't just ...'

A voice suddenly came from the left of me, cutting me off. 'Let her go, Stu,' it said. 'She's made up her mind. You won't change it.' The jangle of jewellery and waft of perfume told me immediately who it was. I turned to confront Wendy looking relaxed, her red caftan flowing all over the lounge chair.

'You! You're the cause of most of this,' I said angrily. 'You and your bloody New Age garbage, filling her head with all those ridiculous ideas.'

She gave me that annoying smile, the one that said she knew something special that I didn't. 'And don't give me that smart-arse look,' I snapped. 'Just go back to fucking New Zealand will you and leave us alone.' I turned away from her and stared slowly around the room. 'I see,' I said, turning in a circle, staring at each stony face. 'It's let's get Stuart time, is it?'

'Stuart, we're all here to help,' said Mary.

'Ha! I know what you mean by help. Shaft me, that's what your idea of help is.'

Mary remained calm. 'I have always said, if you love something you should let it go free and then if it belongs to you it will return.'

'That's the sort of weird philosophical mumb-jumbo I would expect from you, Mary,' I snarled. 'A cart load of your Catholic crap mixed with a bucket load of your daughter's Buddhist bullshit.'

A quiver of fear spread through the group. They had never heard me attack anyone's beliefs with words like that before. I looked again at all their faces. I wanted to retaliate. I clenched my fists.

'You all make me sick,' I said. I looked directly at Jennifer. 'Especially you.'

'Stuart,' came a voice from the edge of the group. It was Tom.

'Oh, the big hero is coming to protect his girl!' I sneered. 'You stay out of this, you fucking prick. I know what you're after, you greedy little bastard.'

'Stuart, please,' chipped in Jennifer.

'He's after my money, that's what he is,' I declared loudly to the room. 'He's thinking that when the divorce goes through half of everything that I've spent my life building up will go to Jenny and he can get his grubby little hands on it. What a bonanza for a layabout musician!' I turned around and lowered my voice to a conspiratorial tone to emphasise my point, nodding towards him. 'None of these bastards ever do any actual work, you know.'

I moved towards Jennifer but Kevin stepped in the way again. I took a deep breath. I was furious. I wanted to smack him one, too. I always had, come to think of it, but the right level of passion and a definitive reason had never been quite in place before. Now I had a good one. However, deep down I knew there was no way around all this. I scanned their faces once more. The odds were heavily stacked against me. When it came to devising an ambush, Jennifer had certainly done her homework. Even Horatio Nelson would have been impressed.

Mary broke the silence. 'Moira and I will help you with the boys,' she said soothingly. 'We'll get through.'

Then came the killer blow. Mum stepped forward, put her hands out and covered my fists. 'Come on Stu, darling,' she said. 'We love you. And we love the boys. It's for the best.'

I could feel the warm, smooth skin of my mother's hands on mine. It felt good. Calming. Comforting. Like when I was a little boy after I had come home from yet another disastrous day in a new schoolyard. It made me feel like I wanted to be cuddled and protected again. I started to shake. The emotion of it all, the discovery of what was going on, the fights, and now the final betrayal, it was all too much. Tears trickled down my cheeks. I unclenched my fists and stepped back. People looked away as I tried to pull myself together.

Then, Wendy got up to leave. Now, there was a turn-up for the books. After all the years of unsuccessfully trying to force her out of my life, I now discovered that all I had to do was turn on the tears and she would have buggered off. 'I don't think it's my place to be here,' she said awkwardly.

'About time you realised that,' I grunted.

I took another deep breath and regained my focus. 'All right, everyone,' I said, 'I get the picture. I've made my bed and now I have to lie in it. Ho, ho, ho!' I giggled loudly, throwing my head back. 'A bit of a bedtime joke there between Jennifer and me.'

No one laughed. Jennifer moved forward. 'Stuart, we're leaving now. Tom and I and Molly are booked on a plane for London. We have to get going right away or we will miss it.'

'Right now? Wow,' I said as the enormity of it all began to hit home. 'Um, okay. I understand.'

I looked around. I could see people were starting to feel relieved that I wasn't going to try and get the drop on big Kev and little Tom and hurl them both through a window.

In the intervening silence, a thought suddenly came to me. I wasn't done yet. 'I'll drive you out to the airport, then?' I offered.

'What?' said Jennifer. I had caught her off guard. 'Ah, no, you don't have to do that.'

'No need, Stuart,' said Kevin, coming up close to me. 'I'm here to do the driving.'

I smiled. The ever-vigilant, ever-protective Kevin had finally found his moment in the sun. 'Ah, the dutiful brother,' I said, patting him on the shoulder. 'Good to see.'

I looked around at the faces and back to Jennifer. 'Well, can I at least go out there with you to say goodbye? Especially to Molly.'

Jennifer looked at her watch. 'We haven't got enough time!' she snapped.

'Please, especially as I won't be seeing her for a while.'

She looked anxiously behind her. Tom hesitated for a moment, then nodded his assent slowly.

'All right,' she said wearily. 'But it will mean we'll have to take two cars. Damn, I just want to get out of here.'

Despite the sparks between the two main protagonists, a sense of relief had come over the bit-part players. People started to relax, unwind a little, murmur to each other. We all went outside. Kevin jogged off down the street and re-appeared a few moments later at the wheel of a brand new BMW, one of those SUV things that lets you sit up high and lord it over all the other drivers. He had hidden it down the road so I would not be alerted to something unusual when I came home from golf. 'Nice car,' I said as I helped load the bags. 'Finally picked a winner at the Curragh, did you?'

171

'Mind the upholstery,' he barked, ignoring the jibe. 'I only picked it up yesterday.' He jumped into the driver's seat. Tom and Jennifer went to climb aboard with Molly, indicating that I would take the boys in the other car. My little daughter looked up at me, her face tired with anguish. The image came back to me! The painting of the sad green-eyed girl on the wall of the manor on our wedding night.

'Can I ride in the car with Molly?' I suddenly blurted. There was silence. I looked down at her gently. 'It would be nice to spend the last few moments with my little girl.'

Jennifer's eyes narrowed. She looked around at the others. Mary shrugged. Tom slowly and unhappily nodded.

'Well, okay, if you must!' snapped Jennifer. 'God, you *love* making things difficult, don't you?'

'What's that supposed to mean?' We were flaring at each other again. 'I've only ever done the best for the family.'

'Ha! Well, you'll have to come with us in Kevin's car. Molly's car-seat is strapped in it and we haven't got time to be mucking around.'

'Tom,' I said, turning to him and throwing him my keys, 'you take the boys and follow in our car. Then after you've flown out, I'll drive them home.' I climbed into the back seat of Kevin's shiny BMW, taking Molly with me. Jennifer, looking very put out, angrily hauled herself into the front passenger's seat next to Kevin. Tom slipped into the driver's seat of my Audi as the two boys scrambled into the rear seat. They both looked wary, perhaps a little scared, but seemed to have some sort of grip on what was going on. I think they figured that once all this drama was over, with Dad in charge of the domestic scene it would be fast food and *The Simpsons* every night.

After a wave of farewell hugs and kisses and streams of tears, Kevin carefully backed his gleaming new vehicle out and, unaccountably, turned left.

'What the hell are you doing?' snapped Jennifer, shocked. 'The motorway's the other way.'

'The M50's blocked,' he said. 'I heard it on the radio. Some eedjit's rolled his delivery van and there's a big game at Croke Park. It's jammed. I know a way to cut across and we'll pick it up further north.'

Jennifer looked at her watch, folded her arms angrily and pushed herself back hard into the plush leather seat. 'We're cutting it fine as it is! We don't want to miss our plane. I couldn't go through all this again.'

'Well,' I said, 'you don't have to, if you come to your senses.'

'Aggh!' she said. 'Kevin, just drive.'

I banged the back of her seat hard with my fist, and then leaned across and checked the seatbelt securing Molly into her booster seat. 'What have we got here?' I said soothingly, pointing to her Hannah Montana backpack. She had books, games, a drink bottle. 'Goin' up in the sky on the big plane, hey?'

Molly looked up at me. Her eyes were sleepy, but she smiled. I had to look away for a second. It was the smile Jennifer first gave me when we met. She was the perfect replica of her mother. Pretty, bright, perky.

I could understand why Jennifer wanted to take her. They were made for each other. They laughed, giggled and played together. They told each other secrets. They cuddled each other when watching television. They were inseparable. Best mates. A unit unto themselves. Apart from our little game of Catch-Molly, they had all but locked me out. 'But,' I thought, 'she is not Jennifer's to take away like this. No, sir. Molly belongs in Dalkey with me, and with her brothers. And with her mother, too, if she chooses.'

I knew Jennifer loved the boys. What mother wouldn't? But boys return love in a different way. They take more than they give and see that as a positive. The fact that you are able to look after them is their own special gift to you. All things considered, it did make sense that they should stay with me. They were almost self-sufficient and with a bit of help from people around – apparently I was going to get the right assistance, according to Mary and Moira – I would be fine. Their lives wouldn't change too much.

But if Jennifer thought she was going to get away with this easily, she had another think coming. She had no right to break up a family. How dare she get involved again with this little jumped up Asiatic drummer boy. How dare she disobey my orders. How dare she organise a gang ambush in my own lounge. With my mother an integral part of the posse, too! What an embarrassing scene. This was humiliating. Well, if she wanted to play rough, then so be it.

21

Determined to prove he had picked the correct route, and perhaps anxious to get Jennifer and me out of his new car as quickly as possible, Kevin drove with a combination of speed to get us to the airport on time and anxiety about not getting his pristine vehicle scratched on the way. In between moments of fuming silence, the pair of us bitched, bickered and screamed at each other, while he scurried along back streets, bounced over kerbs and took us up roads I'd never seen before; which was quite an achievement, because as an insurance salesman, I reckoned I had covered pretty much all of Dublin over the years.

We had barely got to the end of our street when she baited me. She turned around, her voice soft, a little smile on her face. 'Thank you for being so reasonable, Stuart,' she said soothingly.

Reasonable? It was all I could do to resist from leaning forward and grabbing her by the hair, pulling her head back and banging it hard against the seat. 'Bitch!' I hissed. 'It's nothing to do with being reasonable. You rail-roaded me!'

'God damn,' she said. 'See. I try and make peace with you and you still attack me.'

I leaned forward, close to her ear. 'You started all this, Jennifer. Or should I say Jobby?'

She turned around and pushed me in the chest, forcing me back into the seat. 'Go away, you horrible man. I'm glad I'm getting you out of my life.'

'Don't you dare push me around like that,' I snapped, banging on the back of her seat with my fist and making her head rock. 'Don't you worry, I'll still be around. You haven't seen the last of me yet.'

'Cut it out, you two,' Kevin barked suddenly. Jennifer looked at her watch and hissed something under her breath. I sat back. 'This is nothing to do with you, Kevin,' I mumbled.

As he gunned his shiny new toy down highways and byways, followed by Tom and the boys battling to keep up in our car, I stared out the side window, burning with anger. What was that patronising statement Mary had said back there? 'If you love someone, you'll let them go free'? Ha!

Before long, the hum of the car and the emotion of what had happened was too much for little Molly. She dropped off to sleep.

'Been a big day,' I said to Jennifer, nodding down at our little girl.

Jennifer turned around, looked down at Molly, then up at me and then turned back. 'Been a big day for all of us,' she murmured, staring forward.

The quicker Kevin drove, the more anxious Jennifer got. 'Kevin!' she screamed at one stage as we just squeezed through the ever-closing gap between a parked car and a rapidly oncoming plumber's white van. 'You want me to get you there on time, don't you?' he snarled.

'I don't know why you didn't take the motorway,' she yelled.

'I told you, it was blocked and I'll pick it up soon.'

'He knows what he's doing!' I chipped in.

'Don't you back him up,' she turned and said to me. 'I just want to get to the airport and be out of here.' She turned back angrily, folded her arms, pushed herself hard back into the seat again and glared out the side window. 'We'll never make the plane now.'

I turned around and looked out the rear. Tom was really struggling to keep up. I looked down at Molly. She was sound asleep. I looked out the side window. And stewed.

'So,' I thought, 'it has come to this. I'm losing everything I have built up. My home. My family. My wife. Even my daughter.' Now, there was the irony. I loved Molly so much, I could barely bring myself to touch her in case she would break. Sometimes Jennifer saw this as an indication of a lack of feelings for her. That was not true. Our little game of me pretending to drop her and then catch her safely was my one display of affection. But it contained the greatest human element of all. Trust. And for me, trust was everything.

I began to think things through. Molly was as much part of me as the boys were. She was my little girl and I loved her. Yet Jennifer had kept diverting her away from me so that they could form their own little two-person tribe. 'Why should Molly be subjected to all this?' I thought. 'To be made the pawn, the hostage, in Jennifer and Tom's little game?'

I leaned over towards Jennifer.

'You know what?' I said. 'That cocky little smart-arse back there is not Molly's father. I am! I'm her Da! I know what's best for her. And what I say, goes. I'm still the decision-maker. I'm still the captain of the ship!'

'Yeah, well, we're abandoning your precious ship!' Jennifer said. 'I hope you sink in it.'

'That's enough, you two,' yelled Kevin. 'We're almost to the M50.'

I looked out the window to see that the road was beginning to widen and the houses had been replaced by landscaped concrete walls. 'See,' said Kevin triumphantly. 'The motorway's up ahead. I've just got to cross it on this flyover, go down the other side and pick it up.'

He gunned the car up the ramp but as we reached the top and levelled out, there was a mighty screech of brakes and we came to a halt, an anxious Tom pulling up right behind us. 'Feckin' hell,' Kevin muttered. I could barely hear him over the roar of the motorway below. A car up front had stopped and both its front doors were open. The middle-aged driver and his wife were out of their vehicle, bending down anxiously. 'The silly old fecker has hit some eedjit on a motorbike,' hissed Kevin, banging the steering wheel in frustration with his hand. Peering between Jennifer and Kevin, I could just make out the shattered bike and crumpled leather-clad body sprawled across the flyover, blocking our way. The motorcyclist was screaming in pain.

Jennifer turned to Kevin and hit him hard on the arm with a clenched fist. 'I told you to go on the motorway from the fucking start!' she screamed.

'Jennifer!' I said. 'There's no need to swear.'

She turned. 'You! You keep out of this!' she yelled. 'You're the cause of everything. I finally get a chance for freedom, and here you are, sitting right behind me, still bullying me!'

It was her use of the word 'freedom' that really got to me. Everyone was getting their freedom out of this, except me. I would be directly responsible for the boys, with Mary hanging around making sure I did it properly. Not much freedom there. You could bet Kevin and Seamus and the rest of them would be putting their oar in, too. Not much freedom there, either. Not forgetting the input of my mother. Say no more.

Freedom? What a joke. Then it came to me. The only person who truly deserved to be free was Molly. She shouldn't be dragged off to live a miserable life with these two scheming liars. She should be allowed to enjoy growing up with her brothers in her real home. And if not, then she should be allowed to fly free like a little bird. Mary was right – if I love this little one, then I should give her her freedom. The question was, how?

I leaned forward and tapped Jennifer on the shoulder.

'I want to know,' I asked. 'Where are you going to live in London?'

'What's it to you?'

'It's very important to me!' I flared. 'I want to know what situation my daughter is going to end up in. She's being taken away from her beautiful home in Dalkey, so are you going to get a place in Kensington or somewhere decent like that?'

'Well, if you must know, until things sort themselves out, we're moving into Tom's place in Barking Road.'

'Fucking hell, what sort of a life is that? Stuck in some grimy little East End flat with a handful of second-hand toys while you two won't be able keep your dirty hands off each other.'

She turned around angrily. 'Stuart, how dare you!'

'Well, it's true. You're only doing this so you can fuck each other senseless. For the first few months, anyway, until the passion subsides.'

'You bastard!'

'And how will it be for Molly having a drummer for a substitute father?'

'What do you mean? He has a career, he always has plenty of work.'

'Ha! They're notorious those fellows! Their way-out lifestyle. He'll be unreliable, selfish, in and out of work, on the road, a spendthrift. You just see.'

'I trust him.'

'Trust him?! Jennifer, he's let you down once already. Very badly, too. What he did to you when you were young ruined your life for the next twenty years.'

'But he loves me for who I am and wants me for me.'

'Christ almighty, grow up. He wants my money, that's what he wants. And I can tell you, whatever money you do get out of this, sweetheart, and believe me, there won't be much because I am going to fight you to the bitter fucking end, will be gone in a minute on cigarettes and drugs and booze and then you'll be out in the street.'

'I don't want your stinking money, Stuart,' she screamed. 'In fact, I don't want anything from you!'

'Right then! That's a deal,' I hissed, furiously punching the back of her seat. The impact made her head jolt forward and the noise made Molly stir. 'I'll make sure you get nothing at all, Jennifer,' I yelled. 'In fact,' I said, looking down at the sweet little face, 'I'll make sure you lose everything.'

In one quick movement, I leaned across, unbuckled Molly's belt and smoothly lifted her tiny body out of the booster seat. 'Daddy, daddy, what?' she mumbled, still half-asleep.

Without a break, I opened my door and stepped down from the SUV, landing lightly on the flyover, Molly cradled limply in my arms. 'Daddy?' she said drowsily. I looked down at her beautiful face, which started to slowly come alive as I took a couple of steps. 'Are we playing our game?' she said.

Jennifer screwed her head around to see what I was up to, anxiously pushing at the buttons on the unfamiliar console until one finally wound down her window. She stared at me, puzzled, concerned. 'Stuart,' she said very evenly, as if saying it loudly or in a hurried tone might panic me. 'Stuart. What are you doing?'

I stopped, turned around, and stared straight into her eyes. 'You've taken something very special from me,' I said slowly. 'My trust. You found me, used me, and now you're getting rid of me. So now it's my turn to take something special from you.'

'Daddy,' said Molly, 'are we playing Catch-Molly?'

I looked down at her angelic face. 'Yes, darling,' I said, 'yes, we are.'

'Stuart!' screamed Jennifer, as she wrestled with the door handle. 'Stuart!'

'Jennifer,' I said evenly, 'everything comes at a price. Especially freedom.'

I turned away and walked over to the barrier, and with the screams of Jennifer and the roar of the thundering traffic in my ears, lifted Molly high and held her over the edge, like an offering to the gods. She smiled gently up at me, in her trusting little way, as I dropped her. 'Fly free, little bird,' I whispered. 'Fly free.'

Amid the sound of screeching tyres and metal crashing on metal coming from below, I calmly turned around, stared at Jennifer and then at Tom. Then with a military precision that my father would have been proud of, I turned on my heel and started striding briskly away, down the flyover.

As Jennifer's screams pierced through the wall of noise and confusion erupting from the motorway below, my thoughts were quite clear.

'Freedom? Let them enjoy their freedom now.'

THE END

BOOK THREE

Having read Jennifer's view in *Lover, Husband, Father, Monster – Her Story* and Stuart's version in *Lover, Husband, Father, Monster – His Story*, for the chilling finale, read the third book:
Lover, Husband, Father, Monster – The Aftermath.
By Elsie Johnstone and Graeme Johnstone.
Will Jennifer finally get some relief from the devastation she has suffered? Will Stuart seek revenge?

OTHER TITLES

Other works by the same authors include:

- *Our Little Town*, by Elsie Johnstone. A snapshot of life growing up in a small fishing village across four generations.

- *Ma's Garden*, by Elsie Johnstone, a gentle tale about a young couple setting up home and launching a small-town newspaper in 1902.

- *Rainbow Over Narre Warren*, by Elsie Johnstone, the true story of a much-admired priest who built one of Australia's largest parishes through love, trust and respect.

- *The Playmakers*, by Graeme Johnstone, a novel exploring one of the great literary frauds of all time - did Shakespeare actually write Shakespeare?

- *Joan, Child of Labor* - the memoirs of ground-breaking Australian Labor Party politician, feminist, human rights activist and anti-Vietnam campaigner, Joan Child - with Graeme Johnstone.

All books are available as paperbacks or eBooks from amazon.com, smashwords.com, or through online and traditional book retailers.

For more information go to:
www.loverhusbandfathermonster.com

About the author

G raeme Johnstone had a successful career as a journalist, including working for Australia's biggest selling newspaper, The Sun/Herald Sun and writing its popular daily column, A Place In the Sun. Later he and his life partner Elsie established The Wordsmith's Shop, writing material for a variety of clients, before collaborating on the *Lover, Husband, Father, Monster* series. His first novel, *The Playmakers*, was based on the premise that William Shakespeare did not write the plays ascribed to him. His latest works include *Joan, Child of Labor*, the memoirs of one of Australia's most significant women politicians, Joan Child, and *Normie*, a musical based on the 1960s experiences of Australia's first King of Pop, Normie Rowe.

www.ingramcontent.com/pod-product-compliance
Lightning Source LLC
Chambersburg PA
CBHW050403030726
47503CB00006B/1994